CUTIE PIES AND DEADLY LIES

MURDER IN THE MIX 1

ADDISON MOORE

HOLLIS THATCHER PRESS, LTD.

Edited by Paige Maroney Smith
Cover Design: Lou Harper, Cover Affairs

Copyright © 2018 by Addison Moore
This novel is a work of fiction. Any resemblance to peoples either living or deceased is purely coincidental. Names, places, and characters are figments of the author's imagination. The author holds all rights to this work. It is illegal to reproduce this novel without written expressed consent from the author herself.
All Rights Reserved.
This eBook is for your personal enjoyment only. This eBook may not be re-sold or given away to other people. If you would like to share this eBook with another person, please purchase any additional copies for each reader. If you're reading this book and did not purchase it, or it was not purchased for your use only, then please return it and purchase your own copy. Thank you for respecting the hard work of this author.

Copyright © 2018 by Addison Moore

MURDER IN THE MIX

ADDISON MOORE

Cutie Pies and Deadly Lies

BOOK DESCRIPTION

ADDISON MOORE

Cutie Pies and Deadly Lies

My name is Lottie Lemon, and I see dead people. Okay, so rarely do I see dead people, mostly I see furry creatures of the dearly departed variety, who have come back from the other side to warn me of their previous owner's impending doom.

So when I saw that sweet orange tabby twirling around my landlord's ankles, I figured Merilee was in for trouble. Personally, I was hoping for a skinned knee —what I got was a top spot in an open homicide investigation. Throw in a hot judge and an ornery detective that oozes testosterone and that pretty much sums up my life right about now. Have I mentioned how cute that detective is?

Lottie Lemon has a bakery to tend to, a budding romance with perhaps one too many suitors and she has the supernatural ability to see the dead—which are always harbingers for ominous things to come. Throw in the occasional ghost of the human variety, a string of murders and her insatiable thirst for justice and you'll have more chaos than you know what to do with.

Living in the small town of Honey Hollow can be murder.

CHAPTER 1

My name is Lottie Lemon, and I see dead people. Okay, so rarely do I see dead people. Mostly I see furry creatures of the dearly departed variety, who have come back from the other side to warn me of their previous owner's impending doom.

At first, I had no idea what these hologram-like beasts were up to until after an unfortunate run of something akin to trial and error that I concluded each dead pet was some sort of a harbinger for its previous owner, a very,

very bad omen if you will. Sometimes I see them floating around willy-nilly in a crowd and it's hard to decipher exactly who the bad luck is coming for.

But on occasion, I see them attached firmly to the side of whomever the incoming disaster is set to strike. I'm not sure why this is my lot in life. In fact, my lot in life hasn't been so stellar in general. My birth mother thought it was a brilliant idea to leave me on the floor of a firehouse, and that's where a brave and thankfully curious firefighter spotted me, swaddled up and squirming.

It just so happens that I was adopted by that sweet man, Joseph Lemon, and his wife, Miranda, and gifted a book-loving big sister, Lainey, currently Honey Hollow's lead librarian, as well as a feisty and shenanigan-prone younger sister, Meg, who is also known as Madge the Badge on the Las Vegas female wrestling circuit. And being that Las Vegas and all of its glittery wrestling venues are a good distance from Honey Hollow, Vermont, we don't see her very often.

But back to that strange gift of mine, or curse as it more often than not feels—I have zero clue where it came from or why, or even the major significance of it. A part of me has always believed that something alarmingly supernatural occurred around the time of my birth, and that's exactly why my birth mama decided she so desperately needed to offload a seven-pound chunk of bad luck.

The very first time I put the furry-dearly-departed and outright chaos together was when I was seven and I saw the flicker of a barely-there turtle swimming next to Otis Fisher's ear. Later that day, Otis fell from a tree and broke his arm. At the time, I wasn't too sorry about it either. That boy had a mad hankering for pulling on my pigtails. And as fate would have it, the boy who lived to tease me, one day admitted to having a mad crush on yours truly. And post that amorous admission we dated on and off for about three years.

If I thought that boy was annoying in elementary school, he outdid himself in high school. In fact, Otis—or *Bear* as he's affectionately known around these parts for having once chased off a black bear before it could invade and devour an entire herd of innocent tourists who were on a leaf peeping tour—is one of the reasons I left Honey Hollow to begin with. No sooner did my high school diploma cool off than I hightailed it to New York—Columbia University to be exact—where I've had the displeasure to ogle other people's dead pets.

I'm quick to push what I've affectionately dubbed the New York Disaster out of my mind as I take a step outside of my apartment. It's a duplex, actually, and my landlords, the Simonson sisters, live upstairs.

They're the primary reason I'm headed out on this unforgivably crisp September morning wearing my Sunday best, even though it's smack in the middle of the week, Wednesday. Usually, I'd be happily snug in my favorite jeans, sporting my comfiest sweatshirt with my hair in a ponytail, and on my way to the Honey Pot Diner where I'm currently employed as the chief baker, not that there's anyone baking underneath me but, hey, I like the title.

Instead, I'm stuffed in a pencil skirt, two sizes too small, and a blouse that looks as if I swiped it off a mannequin at Goodwill, partially because I did. Okay, so I don't own many Sunday clothes per se, but only because the local church is all about casual attire. They're far more concerned with keeping your soul free from the flames than they are about your accouterments, but I digress.

I'm not headed to work or any holy house in the great state of Vermont. I'm headed to *court*—small claims court to be exact—all the way over in Ashford County.

Just as I'm about to head to my beat-up old hatchback, I spot both the aforementioned Simonson sisters at the foot of the driveway squabbling between themselves about who knows what—most likely me. It is me they're hauling to court after all, and over something completely ridiculous.

It just so happens that last summer at the county fair my blueberry buckle pie won the coveted blue ribbon in its division, and it seemed as if all of Ashford County were thrilled for me, at least all of the townsfolk here in Honey Hollow. But the Simonson sisters were decidedly not enthused in the least.

Sometime between the taste test and the judging, someone edited my entry to read *Simple Simonson Pie* and crossed out the all-important part about the blueberry buckle. Regretfully, a riot of laughter ensued, mostly from the fine, and, might I add, intuitive folk here in Honey Hollow, but I swear on all that is holy that good time only lasted about three thrilling minutes before I made the correction.

Although, to hear Mora Anne and Merilee tell it, the aftermath not only bruised their egos and reputation but managed to cause a retail apocalypse down at the shop they own and run.

It turns out, The Busy Bee Craft Shop was short on patrons and dollar bills alike and had a difficult time paying its rent last month, so the only logical solution they could come up with was to sue me for every last red cent.

Both sisters are dressed head to toe in long velvet coats with ruffled shirts peeking out from underneath like a couple of throwbacks from some long-forgotten steampunk era.

It's eerie the way they choose to dress alike each and every day despite the fact they've been on the planet for twenty-six long years—and twenty-seven respectively. I know this because I happen to be the exact same age as Merilee.

We've all grown up together, but the way they treat me you'd think they were my bitter and scorned elders.

Merilee snarls as if she were rabid. "Well, look who's here? If it isn't Honey Hollow's favorite jester who will soon be performing live in court." Those narrow slits she calls eyes light up like cauldrons. The sisters have always held a witchy appeal to me, what with their long, dark, stringy hair and bony, long fingers. The fact they look as if they suck on lemons day and night doesn't exactly help their plight. "Are you ready to have your bank account turned inside out?"

I scoff at the thought. If they think this is the day they hit a financial jackpot, they'd better think again.

Working shifts at the Honey Pot Diner doesn't afford me much of a bank account. The only thing in my savings at the moment is enough to cover my rent and Pancake's Fancy Beast cat food. I've had Pancake now for over a year, and he officially qualifies as the greatest love of my life.

I glance over to the living room window where he's currently monitoring the situation while licking his paw.

Pancake is a butter yellow Himalayan with a rusty-tipped tail and dart of a line running between his eyes. He is a precious little angel now that he's no longer using my leather ottoman as a scratching post and chewing down all the cables and cords he could get his hungry little paws on. The entire apartment has been cat-proofed, and Pancake hasn't forgiven me yet.

An icy breeze picks up and the row of liquid ambers and maples that lines the street shed the first smattering of red and gold fall leaves. I steal a moment to take in the glory of nature on full display around the two wicked witches determined to make my life a living hell.

Our little corner of Vermont has a habit of turning into a golden and ruby wonderland this time of year, so much so that the leaf peeping keeps the tourists coming in strong right up until winter.

Speaking of tourist traps, the Honey Hollow Apple

Festival is coming up later this month, and I've been asked to supply the pies for the occasion.

After my shift was over at the Honey Pot last night, I baked two dozen personal-sized caramel apple pies—*cutie pies* as I like to call them—and I need to deliver them straight to the orchard this afternoon because the owners requested a sample for their employees. My guess is they want to be sure my baking skills are up to snuff before they live to regret the decision come the day of the festival. But I guarantee they'll far from regret it. In fact, the only thing they might regret is not ordering enough to keep up with demand.

It took me weeks to perfect the right combination of caramel and spices, and I even threw in a handful of crushed walnuts into each tiny pie to give it a little crunch. But it's that buttery caramel that steals the limelight from those golden delicious apples. It's so smooth and creamy, my best friend Keelie and I spent an hour last night licking the bowls clean ourselves.

I can't help but sigh over at the two beady-eyed siblings who relish my financial undoing.

"I won't be having my bank account turned in any direction this morning because there isn't a judge on this planet who would side with—" I'm about to lay into the Simonson sisters with every colorful word in my lexicon when something akin to a flame flickers around Merilee's ankle. For a brief and fleeting moment, I think it's simply a stray leaf, but suddenly that flicker materializes into the clear outline of a long-lost, dearly departed orange tabby that I'm guessing once belonged to one of the shrews before me.

"Ha!" Mora Anne scoffs as she takes a step in close. "She can't finish the sentence because she knows she's guilty. Just admit it and whip out your checkbook. Save us all the trouble of driving to Ashford. We're meeting with Darlene Grand this afternoon to secure a booth for the festival. We don't have a lot of time to dilly-dally with you over a handful of change. Hand it over right now and we can all get on with our day."

I take a moment to scowl at the surly sisters. Since when is three thousand eight hundred dollars a handful of change? And if it's so darn piddly, why bother to sue me to begin with?

The ghostly cat twirls around Merilee's left foot before pausing to look up at me, and I would bet my life that feisty feline just smiled.

The pets I see are never skeletal or gruesomely decomposing but clear as vellum versions of themselves in their plush and fluffy prime. On the rare occasion, I do see a once-upon-a-person, but neither the pets nor the people breathe a single word to me. I'm guessing the lack of vocal cords has something to do with it. And, believe you me, I am more than grateful.

I've only confided my strange gift to one person, and she wasn't family at that.

Nell Sawyer is my best friend's grandmother, and she might as well be mine. She's been that kind to me. If my mother knew about my morbid third eye, she would tie me to a stake and light the flames just trying to usher the dark side out of me. And, well, considering the fact my mother has a way of spreading an errant word around town—you would think she were aspiring to be the biggest gossip Honey Hollow has ever seen—I'm not too sorry I've never broached the subject with her.

But Nell seemed as understanding as she was intrigued, not one ounce of judgment spilled over from that woman. I'm not sure why I told Nell and not my sisters, or Keelie, Nell's granddaughter and my BFF, but something about Nell's sweet round face has the power to pull even the darkest secret from my soul.

"What's the matter?" Merilee chides with a bony hand set over an equally bony hip. "Cat got your tongue?"

I glance down at the curious cute little kitty. "Yes, as a matter of fact, it does. I'm guessing luck is on my side today." *And not yours,* I want to say. "I'll see you ladies in court." I bite down a smile as I give one last look to the tiny poltergeist licking its ghostly paws.

Who knows? Maybe Merilee will trip on the courthouse stairs—and if she does, I hope to see it.

Aw heck, maybe she'll skin a knee.

CHAPTER 2

Ashford County is less than twenty minutes down the highway, and unlike Honey Hollow with its houses tucked against the evergreens, Ashford is more of your urban sprawl, complete with a few high-rises downtown and a nice little brick building next to the courthouse that reads *World's Best Coffee*. And seeing that I have a few minutes to spare, I make a beeline toward that java-laden establishment in hopes to give me the proper energy I'll need to see me through this inglorious day.

But as horrible as getting called to court may be, it's the furthest thing from my scattered mind at the moment. I just can't seem to get over those caramel apple pies waiting for me back at the Honey Pot Diner. I whipped up a few extra so Keelie and the rest of the staff could indulge in the ooey gooey good—

No sooner do I round the corner from the parking structure to the coffee shop than a brick wall of a body crashes into mine.

"*Oh*!" I cry as my purse goes flying as does his briefcase, only to clash all on their own before exploding like a paper filled and blessed by Sephora's finest offerings piñata. A plethora of office supplies and lipsticks rain down over us —in my defense, I had no idea what shade of red went best with a *not guilty* plea, thus the half dozen or so tubes of MAC pelting us like lethargic bullets. "I'm so sorry!" I pant over the dark-haired man with the body of a linebacker already busy scooping up his files posthaste.

"No, it's fine, really," he grumbles as if it were anything but.

"It's not fine. I was so wrapped up thinking about caramel"—I quickly join him in scooping up the eight by ten slices of what feels like an entire Canadian forest sprawled at our feet—"and once I dive deep into the caramel apple pie corner of my mind, I may as well be on another planet entirely."

A tube of lipstick begins to roll toward the gutter, and instinctively I dive over it, slapping it into submission with the palm of my hand. I may not mind secondhand clothes, but I've invested enough into my face to warrant a second car at this point. Nary a lipstick shall be lost on my watch.

I jerk my head up abruptly, and the top of my head hits him in the fun zone a little too hard.

"*Geez*," he howls out in pain as he hobbles backward, protectively cupping his man parts while proceeding to straddle me awkwardly in the process.

"Dear heavens," I pant, struggling to rise and accidentally giving him an inadvertent piggyback ride in the process. "Oh my goodness," I cry as my back begs to cave in from the weight of his body.

"Hang on." His voice rises in an unnatural way as if he were in fact speaking to a horse.

Dear Lord. Kill me. Here I am in the middle of downtown Ashford showing a grown man a bucking bronco of a good time.

"Let's try this another way," I say, dropping flat onto my stomach, and off he rockets, stumbling forward toward a dogwood bush and—oh no, his suit is far too nice to be embellished with twigs.

I grab onto his ankles, and he falls face-first into the border garden, his head and torso buried at least a foot deep in lavender hyacinths.

Okay, so holding onto his ankles wasn't the brainstorm I had thought it would be.

"What the hell did you do that for?" he barks, struggling to right himself.

"Oh dear!" I stagger halfway up just as he backs out and pegs me in the forehead with his rock-hard behind and lands me flat on my back, knocking the wind right out of me.

"Lord Almighty," he grunts, offering me a hand and, soon enough, we're both back on our feet, face to scowling face. His hair is mussed and wild. His eyes are nothing but two irate blue flames, scalding me with their hatred.

"I'm so sorry," I say, my lips quivering as if I were about to cry. My head is pounding, and I feel as if I just crawled through a trench on the front lines, only to make it out half-alive.

"I'm sorry I ever got out of bed this morning." He rakes his fingers through his hair, and it's quickly becoming evident not only did I take down a well-dressed man but I took down an abnormally handsome one at that.

He's smooth skinned, just the right amount of stubble peppering his face, and he looks as if he's got a half-decade on me at least.

"My name is Lottie Lemon, and if you don't mind, I'd love to buy you a cup of coffee for the trouble."

It's the least I could do after giving the front and back of his crotch such an enthusiastic hello with my *face* of all things. Gah!

Once I reiterate this entire fiasco to Keelie, I'm sure this day will go down in infamy as my most proficient foray in testosterone sciences.

"No," he says, heading toward the coffee shop, and I don't hesitate to whiz right next to him, suddenly thrown for a loop because I happened to have thought the shop was in the other direction. That might just be why we bumped into one another so violently.

"What do you mean *no*?" I say, zipping inside as he holds the door open for me and scuttling into the line. "Is that some kind of male machismo thing? Like you can't have a woman buy a cup of coffee for you because it might stick a pin in your ego? Because I'm pretty sure the world has moved well past that point, and I promise you won't suddenly have the need to use a feminine hygiene product just because someone with slightly more estrogen happened to spring for your cup of morning joe. You do realize that men *and* women are comprised of both estrogen and testosterone. In fact, at about the age of seventy, we equal out as far as the aforementioned hormones go, and there's not a lot of gender difference hormonally speaking at that point. But, chances are, I won't be standing next to you to buy that cup of coffee for you when you hit the big seven zero—so, if I were you, I'd take me up on my free latte right now in the present." I step up to the barista waiting to take my order and nod over at him. "I'm buying for the two of us."

"I said no." His eyes slit to nothing.

As if my little Kung Fu takedown outside didn't infuriate him enough—my offer to make all of his java dreams come true has him wanting to rocket through the roof with that briefcase he's clutching as if it had nuclear codes inside of it.

"Fine." I put in my order and pay. And as soon as the barista asks for my name, I say it loud and proud. "L-O-T-

T-I-E"—I turn back at the aggressively handsome, aggressively angry well-suited man and smile—"It's *Lottie*. I'm sorry. I didn't get your name."

"I didn't give it." His lips twitch in the right direction, but there's not a hint of a smile.

So irritating.

I step aside as he puts in his order, keeping an ear open to hear his name once he shouts it over the counter. I just had an impromptu meet and greet with that man's family jewels and had his backside give me a spontaneous high-five over the forehead.

I'm not leaving this establishment until I at least get his initials.

But as fate, or my luck as it were, would have it, the barista doesn't ask. She simply flirts and giggles in his presence as I'm sure women and girls alike are prone to do.

My guess is he's a regular anyways. As soon as my drink is ready, I take my time near the creamers, rearrange the straws and the napkins until his cup lands on the pick-up counter, and then I see it in black and white but don't believe it.

I tiptoe over on the balls of my feet, and my mouth falls open as he scoops it up with pride. He flexes the cup my way so I can get a better look.

"Mr. Sexy?" I flatline.

Gone is the apologetic schoolgirl and come to stay is the hardened-by-life New Yorker that took up residence in me during my short tenure there. Every now and again she likes to make a reprisal and, believe you me, she's a barrel of F-U-N.

"That's right." He gives a subtle wink as he makes his way to the door. "Do yourself and everyone else a favor and watch where you're going, would you? You could walk into a real disaster if you're not careful."

A gasp gets locked in my throat, and I choke on a half a dozen comebacks.

"You watch where *you're* going! And if I were you, I'd consider investing in a jock strap!" Okay, so that's not how I envisioned that would go, but, for whatever it's worth, it felt good to take down his ego a notch.

The barista and—come to think of it—just about every other patron in the establishment is ogling at me as if I just told off the Almighty Himself.

I avert my eyes at the thought. I bet that man was nothing more than some nine-to-five pencil pusher ready to submit to his cubicle prison cell. He's got a sentence of roughly forty years, and I can't say I feel too sorry for him.

I head out the door and up the steps to the Ashford County Courthouse.

Mr. Sexy.

I've got another name for him, and it's not nearly as generous.

THE INSIDE of the Ashford County Courthouse is stunningly opulent with marble flooring, brass hardware, and fixtures. The walls of this particular courtroom they've ushered me into are covered in wood paneling, richly dark and textured like a Hershey's bar.

My mind drifts right back to those mouthwatering cutie pies waiting to be delivered to the orchard this afternoon, and I moan at how decadent they are. There is nothing like a caramel apple on a crisp fall day. There's just something about the buttery caramel sauce, the way the sugar slightly burns my tongue that leaves me wanting more.

Mora Anne coughs and pulls me out of my caramel spell as both sisters sneer at me from the opposite side of the room.

In front of us sits what looks to be a judicial altar with an oversized leather chair waiting for the judge to fill it. The bailiff stands proud at the front of the room, a skinny rail of a man with a nightstick and a scowl.

I can't help but scowl myself. I've never had much luck with men, and this morning has certainly been no different. Here's hoping for a female judge.

He thumps his hands together. "All rise for the Honorable Essex Everett Baxter. Judge Harris is currently unavailable, and he will be filling in for the interim."

Essex? That definitely sounds like a man. An old cranky one. Really, universe? Were a couple of ovaries too much to ask for?

I shoot Mora Anne and Merilee the side-eye for dragging us all to court this morning, including the Honorable Judge Essex Everett Baxter.

I happened to overhear the clerk out front tell the bailiff we were the only case today. If it weren't for those greedy, albeit delusional sisters, we could have all joined Judge Harris for a day off from court.

Mora Anne's mouth falls open, as does her sister's on cue, their gazes both set dead ahead. I glance forward and do a double take as the man in the black robe climbs the stairs and takes a seat.

"Holy SpaghettiOs," I whisper as I take him in. "*Essex*?" I blurt without meaning to. "That's what Mr. Sexy stands for?"

The entire room seems to shut down for three solid seconds before the bailiff responds.

"*Enough*—or you'll be found in contempt. Only speak when spoken to and do *not* interrupt the judge or the plaintiff while they speak their peace."

Mr. Sexy, aka Judge Baxter, picks his own jaw up off the floor. His eyes remain sealed over mine for an undue amount of time, and I can't help but feel a little smugly satisfied by the fact.

Those uptight Simonson sisters are probably deducing far more lascivious reasons that have caused me to garner his handsome as all hell attention, and I can't say I'm too displeased. But I know the real lowdown. Those aren't beams of lust he's shooting my way. More like distrust. Dare I say *contempt*.

"Good morning," he growls my way before nodding over to Mora Anne and Merilee as well.

At least he's an equal opportunity offender as far as his curt demeanor goes. No wonder he didn't have a friendly bone in his body. Law school must have roughed him up just right to land him in that supreme position.

A judge. *Huh*. Never would have guessed. He seems a bit young for the position, but I'm guessing he's plenty old enough to wield that gavel. For a brief moment, I envision him on top of me once again, our noses touching, our lips within firing distance…

He clears his throat as if he were privy to my quasi-lewd thoughts. "Which one of you is Merilee Simonson?"

Merilee raises a hand and with good reason. Essex Everett Baxter may be every bit as scrumptious as that coffee cup suggested, but he is as intimidating as a tidal wave.

He nods. "Okay, you go ahead and tell me what your case is about."

Merilee squares her shoulders. "This case is about the failure to pay my rent on a business my sister and I own to the tune of three thousand eight hundred dollars. You see, the defendant here has made a habit of defaming my sister and me about town—" She pauses a moment to glare at me and a million words beg to trickle from my throat, but Mr. Sexy gives me that *don't you dare* look in his eyes, same one he gave me after I introduced myself to him by way of my forehead this morning, so I don't say a word. "Nevertheless, she went too far last July during the county fair here in Ashford and changed the name of her questionably edible dessert from blueberry buckle to Simple Simonson and turned both my sister and me into a laughing stock."

Mora Anne pumps her fist. "And nobody has set foot in our shop ever since."

Judge Baxter looks decidedly unimpressed with her outburst. "I'm guessing you're the sister?"

"That's it?" I balk. "You're not tossing her in the pokey and throwing away the key? I was assured by your kind bailiff that if I were to have that kind of an outburst—"

His gavel slams over the marble countertop and rings out like a gunshot. "You would be in contempt and, believe me, I'm still considering it," he riots out the words as if I just threatened to set the room on fire.

There it is. It's official. He hates me. I might as well pull out my checkbook right now and save everyone the trouble.

"Now"—he thunders as he shifts his fire and brimstone attention to the Simonson sisters—"do either of you have physical proof that Ms."— he glances down at his paper-work—"Carlotta Kenzie Lemon—"

"Lottie Lemon." I keep it short and sweet and make a zipping motion over my lips before throwing away the imaginary key. I'm sure that right about now he'd like to replace it with a real one.

"Yes," he grumbles, still glaring. No smile. This man is harder to crack than a concrete egg. He takes a deep breath, which I'm guessing is more based on exasperation than it is necessity, before looking back to the Simonson sisters. "Do you have proof that Ms. Lemon instructed your patrons to bypass your business?"

"Yes!" Mora Anne holds her phone out. "I took a picture of the sign myself."

The bailiff takes the phone and hands it to the judge who seems to scowl at it as he seemingly does everything else. "I see."

The phone makes its way back to its rightful owner as Judge Baxter continues to glare at the three of us. "Ms. Simonson." He nods to them both. "Is there any other evidence either of you would like to present?"

Merilee leans in. "I have security footage of an empty store that runs a month straight. That woman singlehandedly dismantled years of good faith relations with the townspeople of Honey Hollow."

The good yet ornery judge closes his eyes a moment too long, a sure sign he's about had enough from all of us. He looks my way and nods. "Let's hear what you have to say for yourself, Ms. Lemon."

"I—" for the life of me I can't seem to put two words together. I'm momentarily both vexed and fascinated by his handsome face, that stubble, and those heated blue eyes.

"I think that this is all a load of malarkey." Bullcrap is more like it, but who knows where that quasi-salty word might land me. "I swear under oath and on a stack of Bibles that I wasn't the one who crossed out the words *blueberry buckle*. Nor did I alter in any way the name of the dessert I toiled over. It took me four months to perfect that recipe.

And, I also swear on all that is holy that I don't have a clue who wrote the words *Simple Simonson* on that index card. I'm innocent, Your Honor. This is all a very bad mix-up. And, as you might be well aware, I'm pretty good at getting myself in a tangle or two." His eyes widen a notch just as a thought comes to me. "Hey, wait a minute." I turn to the spoiled sisters and their gnarled expressions. "I happen to work across the street at the Honey Pot Diner, so I guess you could say I'm privy to the foot traffic on Main Street. If you say you've lost all of your customers due to the fact I've poisoned all of Honey Hollow against you, how do you explain the fact that you haven't had a single tourist stop by?" I turn my attention to those startling blue eyes. "I say this, Your Honor, because the only thing keeping the cogs in our wheels turning down on Main Street is the change that lines those tourists' pockets. If they have footage that proves their store has been empty for a month, well, I've had nothing to do with the fact the tourists aren't pouring in like they used to—just like I don't have anything to do with the fact the residents have fled the scene. I'm innocent, and this is all a load of pot-crockery that's wasting your valuable time and mine. I don't think I should pay them a single dime."

He smacks his lips. "The commentary at the end was completely unnecessary." He turns to the sisters. "Normally, this is where I would pause to consider the facts, make up my mind, and deliver a judgment. But since the fact this case is solely built on slander—and absolutely no proof that the defendant caused it to begin with, your entire case rests on hearsay and speculation. This case is dismissed. Ms. Lemon, you are absolved from the accusations."

I suck in a quick breath and clap, silently yet enthusiastically. "Thank you," I say and give an awkward wave as he abandons his post.

Mora Anne and Merilee head over, sour-faced, tight-lipped, and beady-eyed. I can feel their wrath as sure as a furnace.

"Isn't that nice?" Mora Anne's lips expand like a rubber band. "Make cute with the judge and, sure enough, he sides right along with you."

Merilee sniffs my way. "Well, you can start packing." She hands me a thin manila envelope. "This is your official eviction notice."

"I'm being evicted? On what grounds?" Need I ask? Really?

"Our cousin is moving in the first of October."

"But that's in less than three weeks. Where will I go?"

"That's not our problem." Mora Anne giggles as they exit, and for the first time since I've known her, it seemed genuine. Figures.

It takes a full five minutes, and the pointing finger of the bailiff for me to find the exit. The marbled hall is empty save for the laughter of a female and the murmurings of a man, and just as I'm about to round the corner to leave, I bump into Judge Baxter, although far less violently than before.

"Geez." He takes a full step back and holds an arm over

his lady friend as if to shield her from my gravitational pull. Probably a smart maneuver on his part.

"Thank you once again, Mr. Sex—um, *Essex,* or um, Judge Baxter," I say sheepishly before glancing to the sleek and polished brunette by his side. She's wearing a royal blue power suit, and those heels she's walking on have to be at least six inches tall. My own feet hurt just looking at them. Her face is smooth and heavily made up as if she just had a professional airbrush her into oblivion. Her lips are understated, not a garish shade of red in sight, and yet that shade of judgment in her eyes isn't exactly appealing.

He offers a curt nod. "You're welcome. And it's Everett. I go by Everett. I don't expect to see you on the inside of my courtroom again, Ms. Lemon."

"Oh, you won't—*Everett.* In fact, if you're lucky, you won't see me at all, ever again!" A tiny twinge lives and dies deep in my belly as if it mourned the fact.

He frowns at the thought. "Have a good day. And, please, for your own sake, watch your step."

Both he and the brunette are careful to make their way around me as she giggles against his shoulder.

"Essex, what's this Everett business? Don't you ever con me into calling you that."

"I think you know just what to call me and when," he growls back with a dark laugh of his own.

I clear my throat and wave until I've managed to garner his attention once again.

"Essex, Mr. Sexy, Everett, Judge Hard-as-Flint, whoever you are—I'm glad you were in that courtroom today." Both he and his paramour go slack-jawed before taking off once again. "Too bad you don't have the ability to straighten out the rest of my life," I whisper, mostly to myself. "I'm so steaming mad at Mora Anne and Merilee I could wring their necks."

Everett turns around and glances my way before they disappear down the hall.

And to think Merilee didn't have the courtesy to skin a knee.

The day is young yet.

CHAPTER 3

"Lottie Lemon, I never knew you!" Keelie Nell Turner moans as she digs a fork into a half-eaten cutie pie. "I swear on the Honey Pot's dusty soul, I have never tasted anything so decadent in all my life. And are those walnuts I'm loving so much?"

"They are," I say, putting my purse into a cubby in the back of the kitchen before heading to the baking nerve center of the Honey Pot, my own personal domain, as I like to call it. I do a once-over for the pies I set out, but they've up and disappeared. "Please tell me you didn't eat that stack of goodness I had ready to deliver to Holland Grand at the Orchard."

"I wish." Keelie rolls her eyes, her lashes batting away a mile a minute as she moans through another bite.

Keelie has been my best friend as long as I can remember. And her twin, Naomi, has been my nemesis since about the eleventh grade. Naomi had a thing for Bear at the time, and Bear had a thing for me. By and large, Naomi has never done well with not getting her way. One would think her hatred for me stemmed from far more close to home reasons, like the fact Keelie and I were inseparable since preschool. But Naomi has her own best friend, and she's just as snooty as Naomi is.

But both Naomi and Keelie are gorgeous lookers, born with long blonde curls right out of the womb—Naomi has since dyed hers black, blue eyes for days, and a smile that could illuminate the Western Hemisphere—just Keelie, that is. Naomi is made of piss and vinegar, and that's precisely why I go out of my way to avoid crossing paths with her. She runs the Evergreen Manor, the one and only inn at the foot of town, and it's a shocker she hasn't scared away all the tourists by now.

"You've outdone yourself, girl." Keelie dips her pinky into the caramel sauce and licks it clean. "Forget working for the Honey Pot. We need to open up a pie stand. This stuff is G-O-L-D."

"Quit the Honey Pot?" the voice of an elderly woman sings from behind, and both Keelie and I turn with a laugh caught in our throats because we'd recognize that sweet voice just about anywhere.

"Nell!" I'm the first to throw my arms around the woman I couldn't love more if she were family. Keelie piles on, and poor Nell is left gasping for air until we land back on our feet.

Nell looks every bit the Queen of England with a dark maroon coat and matching pillbox hat. Her white little curls have been carefully coifed, and she has a smidge of pink lipstick on to boot.

Nell is the one who gifted Pancake to me exactly a year ago. She went over to a breeder in Leeds to pick out a Himalayan for herself and couldn't decide between two brothers and wound up taking them both. She said she'd let me keep one if I simply took one home. I suggested she keep the brothers together, but Nell insisted she just wanted the one. So we named the tiny fluffy kittens together. Pancake and Waffles.

I can't help but think the fact our cats are siblings somehow bonds us that much more.

Keelie gives her hat a quick tap. "Grammy, where are you headed all dolled up like this? You're not headed to the senior center trolling for another boyfriend, are you?"

I can't help but chuckle. Nell might be ninety-two, but she's still pretty spry, and that boyfriend thing is no joke. About six months ago, she took up a suitor, and he took her out to dinner at the fancy Italian place across the street and everything. The entire town was in a tizzy.

"I may. May not." She winks my way. "Actually, I came

to check up on things." She looks around the inner workings of the diner she's owned for going on fifty years. A tiny cough bubbles from her, and she's quick to cover her mouth. "Oh Lord, get me out of here before they shut the place down because I've croaked in the kitchen."

Keelie gives me the side-eye. Nell has made a habit of trying to predict her demise. Much to our delight, she's wrong every single time.

She tousles Keelie's hair as best as she can, and even with that Keelie only looks better. Now it's me giving her the side-eye.

"Your mother is down the street at the bank, so I've only got a minute." She looks my way. "Why don't you ladies walk me out front before I trip over a dishrag or slip in a grease puddle? You know I'll have no one to sue but myself."

"Sure thing," I say as Keelie and I each thread an arm through hers and lead her proudly through the kitchen into the Honey Pot proper, which is already decorated for fall with red and gold silk leaves lining the windows, a miniature pumpkin on each table, and a life-sized scarecrow with the cutest little smile that the tourists can't stop taking selfies with at the entry.

The Honey Pot isn't your typical greasy spoon. We serve only the best comfort food you can find. Both Margo and her husband, Mannford, are chefs who used to work in a fancy revolving restaurant in Manhattan, but left city life about six years ago. Ever since they've been working their magic at the Honey Pot, we've received write-ups from just about every national newspaper and have even been featured on the Good Eats network as a noteworthy stop to visit.

Keelie leads the way outside, and the cool September air kisses us unrepentantly. I traded my flip-flops for boots about two weeks ago.

Fall has a habit of arriving just a touch early in these parts, and not one person is the slightest bit angry about it. Our summers can be as hot as our winters are frozen. As my mother likes to say, *you can always put on another sweater, but you can't take off your skin.* As grisly as that sounds, Miranda Lemon is a lot of things, and right is always one of them.

The sound of hacksaws and jackhammers steals the tranquility that Main Street typically holds, and we look next door to find the old vacant deli being gutted by none other than my grizzly ex, Otis Bear Fisher. Once he spots the three of us, he stops that bandsaw he's close to shaving off his fingers with and heads on over.

"Hey, Bear." I give a half-hearted wave.

Bear and I are on pretty good terms. He's still convinced there's something between us, and I'm still convinced there's not enough air space in the world to create a proper buffer. But he's just as happy-go-lucky as he was when he was a kid. Nothing or no one, and that includes me, can sour his mood.

He offers me a great big hug before pulling back with that toothy grin he's known for. Bear is tall and handsome, blond, and tan most of the year, even though our little corner of Vermont rarely sees that ball of gas otherwise known as the sun.

His good looks keep the girls coming in strong, and lucky for Bear, he's learned the fine art of keeping them all on a rotation. There was a little scuffle for his attention last year, and there might have been fists flying—between the girls. Yes, Bear is very much in demand, just not by me.

"What do you think, ladies?" Nell tips her nose at the plume of drywall dust blooming out the door. "What kind of a shop would you like to see go in next door?"

Keelie's eyes grow wide. "A tattoo parlor and we can come over with pies and take a look at the beefcakes walking around this place. Lord knows I haven't had me a good slice of beef—"

Bear grunts as he cuts her off, "How about a bar? You can't get a decent drink on Main Street. As it stands, the boys and I have to drive down to Leeds to wet our whistles."

"Not a bar." I avert my eyes at the thought. I know first-hand what kind of bars Bear and the boys visit when they head down to Leeds. His cousin, Hunter, yes, Hunter Fisher—his mother has quite the sense of humor—anyway, Hunter took my side in our messy breakup and informed me there were a few places in Leeds where a hormone hungry man like Bear could get his appetite filled in more ways than one. "How about a bakery?" My heart thumps wild in my chest at the prospect. "I could run it for you, and I'd happily bake my heart out to make all the tasty treats that place could ever need or want."

A squeak comes from Keelie as she looks forlorn. "You can't leave me. We're a team, remember? Once you came back from New York, you said we'd never be apart again."

"I'll be next door."

"With a wall between us." She gives a slight wink because she loves to get me going. Keelie is only slightly kidding. We've appreciated every minute we've gotten to spend together at the Honey Pot.

Otis plucks a hammer from his tool belt and points it at the window next to me. "I can bust a hole through the wall and connect the two together. Sort of a walkway."

I gasp at the thought. "Who said you weren't full of bright ideas?"

"You." His lids close just enough to let me know he's smoldering for me, and I can't help but laugh.

The sound of a car horn goes off, and soon Otis is helping Nell into the passenger's seat of Keelie's mother's Town Car.

"I'm all for the bakery!" Nell calls as Otis is kind enough to buckle her in. "You'll have to get the equipment. I don't know anything about that, but my guess is it's more than a pretty penny. You'll need a loan if you can get one. We can work out the details some other time!"

They take off, and Otis blows me a kiss before heading back to the disaster zone next to the Honey Pot.

"I'm going to need a loan? There's not a person in their right mind who'll give me two nickels to rub together."

"How about your mom?" Keelie wrinkles her nose because the answer is clear before either of us verbalizes it.

"She's already struggling to keep the B&B alive and kicking. I keep telling her to raise her rates, but she's afraid she won't be able to compete with the Evergreen and all those sales they keep having—buy two nights get one free."

It's true. My mother's bed and breakfast has been struggling since Naomi took the helm down at her only real competition, the Evergreen Manor. Lucky for Mom, there's a surplus of tourists this time of year, so it doesn't seem to matter.

"Sorry." She winces.

"It's not your fault. And probably not your sister's either." Like heck it isn't. There's no doubt in my mind Naomi has taken the vendetta she has against me and extended it to my mother.

Keelie's eyes light up like torches. "I have an idea." She spins me around until I'm facing the south end of the street and gives me a firm shove. "Get that loan right now, Lottie Kenzie Lemon! There's no time like the present." She scuttles me down a few yards further until my feet start in on a forward motion of their own. "Go on. Right now head into that savings and loan, and don't you leave until they're throwing dollar bills at you!"

Shockingly, my legs keep up with the farce. "But I didn't get to tell you about Mr. Sexy! And have I mentioned I'm getting evicted?"

"You can live in the bakery!" she shouts back. "Or with Mr. Sexy! Better yet, give him to me for safekeeping!"

I'd laugh if I thought at all it was funny. Everett Baxter is far too ornery for either my best friend or me.

NO SOONER DO I get into the bank than I get tossed right back out. It turns out, the loan department is having a few renovations of their own, so in the interim, the loan department is taking up residence in a small office next door. I take a quick breath before staring at the dismal looking box of an entry.

I can't believe that I, Lottie Lemon, am going to have the moxie to walk up to some poor financially bound soul and ask for a piece of the monetary pie. It's not like me. It's dangerous. It's daring. It's downright exhilarating is what it is.

"Unique New York. Unique New York. Unique You *Nork*."

Drats.

I always botch that up.

It's an old vocal exercise I used to employ whenever I went on an interview when I actually lived in the city—and I did go on my fair share of those. Suffice it to say, I didn't get a sweet, tasty bite of that big red apple. Instead, it was rotten and mushy, and I ended up with the worm of the bunch. But enough about my exes for one day.

I head on in and find a comely man who looks to be a little older than me in a baby blue dress shirt sitting behind the desk looking up at me wild-eyed before springing to his feet. His eyes are the color of fresh spring grass, and there are two comma-like dimples that dig in on either side of his cheeks despite the fact he doesn't look happy to see me in the least.

I'm guessing he hates the hole they've stuck him in. I'm pretty sure there aren't too many people vying for loans in Honey Hollow. Come to think of it, that might actually work in my favor.

"Lottie Kenzie Lemon." I extend a hand, and he offers up a warm, firm shake. Something about the way he looks at me while doing so sends a dizzying wave of delight right to the pit of my stomach, but I'm betting that's less an instant attraction I'm feeling and more bats in the digestive belfry ready to vomit out of me. I've never asked for anything in my life, let alone a bouquet of dollar bills.

"Noah Corbin Fox." He motions to the plastic lawn chair in front of me, and we both take a seat. "How can I be of service to you today?"

"You sure can be of service to me!" That wave of nausea gets a bit stronger, but it's not my breakfast I'm about to hurl up between us. It's an entire ocean of words I can feel bubbling to the surface. It's a bad habit I have. When I get nervous, I get chatty. I'll talk about how bright the sun is or how dark the dirt is. It doesn't even matter if the words string together in cohesive sentences so much as it does that my vocal cords are doing their job. "I went to court this morning and won. My landlords, the Simonson sisters, have had it in for me for quite some time. They hate me something awful, but don't you feel sorry for me. The feeling is mutual. Mora Anne used to be in charge of the cheerleading squad at Honey Hollow High, and I was her minion. Boy, did she ever try to drill sergeant me to death. But I won us the trophy in the tri-city competition, and I swear on all things delicious that she's been even angrier with me ever since. And Merilee? I could strangle her with my bare hands for accusing me of hurting their business and turning the last few weeks of my life into a constant stream of worry. She's the one that pointed the accusatory finger at me first."

"So, did you kill her?" He leans back in his chair, looking every bit amused.

"No sir, not yet." I give a cheeky wink. "But the day is young, as my deceased father liked to say." Dear goodness, am I really leveraging the death of my poor father in hopes to garner an ounce of pity from this city deployed loan officer? "My guess is you're from the city since I've never seen you around these parts before. I know just about everyone in Honey Hollow, having grown up here all my life—with the exception of that one time I flew the coop and found myself knee-deep in Manhattan. I went to school there—business school at Columbia. After my mother died, my father made sure." My hand clips my lips. "Dear Lord, did I just curse my mother? I meant to say after my *father* died my *mother* made sure each of her girls received a proper education. She never wants for us to depend upon a man. She says they tend to walk out or die, and that only the very lucky find a keeper with a good ticker." He winces. "Anyway, getting back to all things delicious —I was sort of hoping you'd like to go into business with me. I'm a pretty decent baker, and there happens to be a nice storefront available right next door to the Honey Pot." My entire body breaks out into a sweat at once. "What do you say?"

He gives a long, tired blink, and I can't help but note he looks decidedly handsome while doing so. That's two for two today on the sexy front. First, Mr. Sexy himself, then this tall, dark, and handsome glass of cold—

"No."

"Excuse me?" I blink back to life.

"I said no." His dimples dig in as if mocking me. "I'm not interested. I have no vested interest in baked goods other than eating them, so I'm going to have to pass." He pulls a stack of files forward and straightens them. "Now if you'll excuse me, I've got a business of my own to tend to."

"*What?*" I screech so loud I don't even recognize my own voice. "But that's what you do. You lend money. Look, I know my employment history is a bit shaky, but in all fairness, we haven't even gotten that far. And secondly, you have absolutely zero compassion to be in this line of work." I stand to leave and accidentally knock the plastic lawn chair out from underneath me.

He comes around quick, and we both bend over at the same time to right it, giving our heads a hearty knock in the process. A guttural *oof* emits from him.

"My word!" I back up, stunned. "I think I'm seeing stars."

"Here, take a seat." He pulls the chair up behind me, but I'm quick to evade it.

"And listen to your kind refusal of my more than

enticing offer? No thank you. Do you know what a bakery could do for a town like this? You may not have been here for five hot honey minutes, but we happen to *thrive* off tourism. And believe me when I say that tourists like and require their fair share of sweet treats. An entire store devoted to tasty confections is exactly the missing piece to Honey Hollow's economical puzzle." I go to take a step to my right, and he does so along with me. A slight smile tugs at his lips, and it infuriates me to witness it. "Get out of my way, Mr. Fox. I'm heading straight back into that bank and informing them of your rude demeanor."

I take off as he gives a dark chuckle. "You do that!" he calls after me.

I hightail it right back into the savings and loan and hightail it right back out once they assure me the ornery Fox next door is not in fact employed by their fine establishment. It turns out, the loan department was on my other left.

My phone goes off, and I pluck it out of my purse. It's a text from Holland at the orchard. They'd like to discuss my pies.

I glance back at the window to my left and glare at the obnoxious, albeit handsome, man still rocking away in his seat.

It's been a full day of smug men. Let's hope Holland isn't one of them.

CIDER GROVE ORCHARDS is to die for this time of year. There is no season like autumn in Vermont, and autumn in Honey Hollow is the jewel in nature's crown.

The birch trees shudder in the cool breeze, and the maples and liquidambars shed batch after batch of leaves in a colorful patchwork over the ground. Pumpkins of every size and color dot the entry to the orchard as I get out of my car and take in the scent of evergreens mixed with the apple orchard in the distance.

My mother would bring my sisters and me here each and every September since we were little girls. The Grands have owned this place going as far back as time, and every school in all of Vermont has trekked up here at least once to experience the field trip of a lifetime.

I head over to the old rustic barn they've converted into an office, and just as I'm about to head into the structure, the sound of women squabbling garners my attention. To the side of the building I spot Mora Anne and Merilee with their hands on their hips while they have it out with a few women I recognize from my mother's walking group. Chrissy Nash, the mayor's ex-wife—they recently divorced because he cheated. It was quite the scandal.

Next to her stands a red-faced Eve Hollister—she's in charge of the book club my mother is a part of. It's more spice than it is anything nice, but not a single one of those women has ever complained about the content of those romance novels that keep them up at night. And there's yet a third woman I can't quite make out. She looks vaguely familiar, but I'm not sure I've seen her around town before.

Huh.

I head inside and find the secretary who lets me know that Holland is out back, so I make my way in that direction. Holland is a year younger than me—the youngest of three boys and two girls. For a while he dated my sister, Meg, but that petered out pretty quickly. Lainey swears that's the reason she ran off to Vegas, but I've never given the theory much credence. Meg has always been a spitfire in every capacity. Some people will simply combust if they stick around in a small town like Honey Hollow. And Meg was about to explode into matchstick pieces. It was safer all around for anyone that she took off to sow her wild oats.

From the back of the property I'm treated to sweeping views of the orchard where all you see for miles are bright green trees dotted with beautiful apples in every shape and color, hanging like Christmas tree ornaments, proud and ripe for the picking. I snuggle into my flannel a moment, thankful I went home to change into something far more appropriate to run wild at the orchards.

As soon as I wrap up my meeting with Holland, I plan to pick an entire bushel of apples myself so I can whip up another batch of cutie pies to sell at the Honey Pot.

"Holland?" I call out as I head toward the orchard to my left.

There's a tiny white sign that reads *Jonagold,* and I'm instantly in love with the peachy-yellow blushed little bulbs. I pluck the first one I see right off the branch and rub it against my flannel before sinking my teeth into its delicious goodness.

I just know Holland won't mind. I can't help it. They're so lush and amazing to look at and, dear Lord up in heaven, is this ever so sweet and juicy.

I take a quick stroll through the grounds, enjoying every delicious bite of the quasi-forbidden fruit as thoughts of this psychotic day filter through my mind.

There are some days in Honey Hollow that seem to go by in the blink of an eye and some that last forever. I'm pretty glad this blue-skied beauty of an afternoon falls in the latter category. Before long I head back toward the barn and spot a smattering of people on the other end of the orchard. The flatbed they use to haul the tourists around in is chock-full of people, and I bet that's Holland there in the driver's seat.

The sound of footsteps rushing by steals my attention, and it's only then I note an entire display of my cutie pies on the left side of the building. Almost every last one is gone save for a few in the back, and I can't help but feel a smidge of satisfaction knowing they couldn't keep their hands off my pies.

I head over, anxious to have a quick bite myself. Those Jonagolds are delicious, but they'd be a heck of a lot more decadent slathered in caramel sauce. Just as I'm about halfway to the display table, a long, dark tendril lying over the ground stops me cold.

We don't get snakes this time of year—do we? But it's

not a snake. It almost looks like... *hair*? I make my way over cautiously, fully expecting to find a scarecrow turned on its ear, or a scarf that Mora Anne or Merilee whipped up with their *witchcraftery*, a term Keelie and I came up with a long time ago. I take a few more cautious steps forward and gasp. That's no snake, and there's not a scarf in sight.

It's one of the Simonson sisters, facedown in one of my cutie pies. And judging by that pool of blood she's lying in, she won't be needing a scarf ever again.

She's dead.

CHAPTER 4

In a matter of moments my screams cut through the silence, sending a dizzying blur of people running this way, and before I realize it, a thick crowd blossoms around me from out of nowhere.

Mora Anne stalks my way, white as snow. "You did this! You killed my sister!"

"No." I shake my head, my voice hardly audible as she dives back into the crowd and screams *my sister, my sister* over and over again.

It feels like moments drift by all too quickly, and at the same time it feels like an eternity, but before I know it, Keelie is standing before me, blinking into my face, her lips moving, but I can't quite get a grip on what she's saying. It's all moving way too fast.

The familiar frame of a man speeds in this direction. "Everybody back! This is a crime scene. All of you out of the area *now*," he bellows, and it's only then I snap out of my daze long enough to realize it's Noah Fox, the one I had mistaken for a loan officer not less than a couple of hours ago.

Keelie offers me a quick embrace. "I'd better help Holland wrangle these people into the barn. Better yet, get them off the property." Police sirens cut through the chaos, and she points back at the road. "Daddy's already here. Everything is going to be okay."

She takes off, and I breathe a sigh of relief as the crowd dissipates right along with her. Keelie's father is the chief of the Ashford County Sheriff's Department. He and Keelie's mother divorced years ago, and a few weeks back there was a short-lived rumor he was dating Mayor Nash's ex-wife.

"Hey"—Noah Fox speeds my way and gently lays a hand on my shoulder—"you look a little pale. Why don't we get you over to the barn with everyone else? I'll be here until the police arrive."

"No, I'm not okay. And I'm not leaving. Merilee was my"—I pause a moment—"well, I guess I can't call her a friend. It wouldn't be right to lie about the dead. But she was my landlord right up until she handed me an eviction notice this morning. Besides, I'm the one that found the body. *Body.*" I shudder at the thought of anyone I know being relegated to such grisly terms. I blink up at him a moment. "And what are you doing here? Last I saw, you were gloating at your desk."

He whips out his wallet and flashes a license of some sort at me. "I'm a private detective." He casts a suspicious glance around the vicinity. "I'll be investigating the homicide along with the sheriff's department."

"What? How do you know that? And how did you get here before the police? A private detective?" It comes out with disbelief. "I'm assuming that means you need to be hired. You're like some seedy ambulance chaser, only with dead bodies. Oh my goodness"—I duck out from his grasp—"you're not the killer, are you? Not that I'd expect for you to admit it."

He frowns and looks decidedly handsome in the endeavor, causing my heart to thump just once. Talk about guilt. My heart should not be thumping with lust while poor Merilee's heart can't even give a weak beat.

"I heard it over the scanner." He looks over his shoulder as a small army of patrol cars race up onto the property. "Look, I'm going to take this one on pro bono. I need to prove myself before I can build a clientele. Besides, I've worked for seven years as a homicide detective in Cincinnati."

"Cincinnati?" It comes out faint, mostly because I was just parroting it back to myself.

Captain Jack Turner stalks over with his hand on his weapon, inspecting poor Merilee just as Mora Anne comes racing back to the scene.

"She did it!" Mora Anne is quick to point a finger in my direction. "She killed my sister. We took her to court and gave her an eviction notice this morning and now my sister is *dead*!" she screams those last few words out hysterically.

And suddenly I feel like screaming out my innocence in the exact same manner.

"I didn't do it, I swear!" I cry over to him, and Jack makes a motion with his hand for me to calm down.

That even-tempered look on his face lets me know he fully believes me. And I know that he does. When my own father died, Joseph, the man who found me in the firehouse —it was Jack who stepped in and treated me like one of his own.

"What are you doing here, Lottie?" Jack asks, looking every bit exasperated as beads of sweat quickly build on his upper lip and under his eyes.

I've seen him sweat buckets for less. It's simply the way his body reacts to life. Lord knows it's not nearly hot enough to break a sweat today—never mind that it won't be until next summer. Honey Hollow loves its winters so much sometimes it feels as if it never wants to let go.

"I—I came by to see if they liked the pies I made for them." I glance down at poor Merilee with her face still buried in one. "Holland Grand hired me to bake all the pies for the Apple Festival in a couple weeks, and I wanted to see if they were a hit. I couldn't find Holland, but I found her." My hand clamps over my mouth as I look back to where Mora Anne kneels at her sister's side, the blood around Merilee's torso quickly drying to a dark shade of brown.

"I see." Jack's chest expands wide as the sky. "And how about you, son? What business do you have around these parts?"

Noah shoots those lawn green eyes my way, and I swear on my father's grave I'd like nothing better to do than stare into them the entire livelong day. How in the heck I got myself wrapped up with a dead Simonson sister is beyond me.

"I'm with her." Noah nods my way.

That dark hair of his catches the light, and it looks glossy and soft enough to touch, but I resist the urge. At this point I should probably resist the urge to breathe. Lord knows what trouble I might find myself in next.

"With her?" Jack looks amused. He's quite the intimidating sight in his tan uniform, his badge blinding us like a distress signal every few seconds.

He's a husky man, tall as a tree and round as a barrel. Has a soft look in his eyes that could make even the most hardened criminal feel a slight inkling of affection.

"Yes, with her." Noah nods to me, and that slight comma-like dimple goes off. I've always been a sucker for a good dimple, but something tells me if I'm not careful, my love for those epidermal impressions might land me in the morgue next to Merilee.

"And how do you two know one another?" Jack narrows his gaze at Noah first, then me.

"We're dating." Noah lands an arm around my shoulder. "It's something new. Very new." He looks to me pleadingly and nods. "We were just talking about some kitchen appliances I was going to see if I could help her out with." He gives a long blink and sorry nod as if it were true on some level.

A gasp gets caught in my throat. For the second time in a short span, I can't help but feel guilty about being excited about something while standing feet from the deceased.

"Yes," I say firmly while glaring at Noah. "It's very *new*. It's so new I hardly know about it myself. He's with me," I concede.

"Fine." Jack looks back to the scene as deputies and firefighters alike swarm over the vicinity. "Since you found the body, they'll want a statement from you. Don't go anywhere." He glowers at Noah for a moment. "That goes for the both of you." He takes off, and I pull Noah off to the side.

"Are you insane? On second thought, don't answer that. I already know the answer. You know they probably have this entire place under surveillance. If you're the killer, they're going to find out soon enough and *arrest* you." My goodness, how I hope they have this entire place under a scrutinizing technological eye. I give a quick glance to the bare eaves and it looks doubtful. "What are you, anyway?" I look back to this fake loan officer turned PI. "Some serial killer from the big city? Cincinnati ran out of places to hide, so you chose Honey Hollow as your next foxhole? Nice fake last name, by the way. I bet the first one's a fake, too." I poke him in the chest with my finger and can't help but note he's hard as a rock.

"No." He gives a halfhearted laugh. "I promise you I'm no such thing. I'm telling the truth about my time on the force."

He winces over at the officers working in earnest just as a white van marked *coroner* rolls onto the scene.

"Oh my word. It's all so real." I shake my head just as Keelie materializes between us.

"Everything okay?" She shakes her head at me as if it's not, and it isn't. "What's this my dad is spewing about a boyfriend of yours?" She looks to Noah, and her affect smooths out. "Hot honey on a cool autumn day." She extends her hand. "Keelie Nell Turner, I work at the Honey Pot and am off by eight on Fridays." She gasps a moment, retracting her hand before he can shake it. "You're not the boyfriend, are you?"

"He is," I say, fully annoyed, craning my neck over her shoulder as one of the sheriff's deputies rolls out the bright yellow caution tape just the way they do on TV. I can't believe poor Mora Anne has to witness all this.

"I am indeed the boyfriend." He gives a quick grin. "Noah Fox." He shakes her hand, and Keelie swoons as if she's just met a celebrity.

Keelie gasps again. "Holy stars up in heaven, Lottie! How in the heck did you pull this scrumptious rabbit out of your hat?"

She looks genuinely stunned, so I swat her on the arm to break the spell.

Noah steals a moment to gloat. “It’s new.”

“It’s not new.” I swat him, too. “Would you stop saying that? We are not new. And we never will be. There is no *we* for goodness’ sake!”

Keelie gasps again. I swear, if she does it one more time, she’s going to pass out. “Are you Mr. Sexy?” Her eyes grow wide. “Lottie mentioned you this afternoon.”

Noah gives another smug grin, his chest expanding wide right along with his ego.

“He is *not* Mr. Sexy.” I give a slight push to his arm. “I thought he was a loan officer. It turns out, he’s nothing but a *fake detective*.” I hop on my toes as I hiss the words at him.

“I’m licensed in the state of Vermont.” He looks over to the crowd. “Which reminds me, I have a crime scene to tend to. Ladies.” He offers a slight wink my way, and I can’t help but groan with frustration.

“This entire day is a mind warp. How can any of this be happening?”

“I know, right?” Keelie stares off into the orchard, dazed as if trying to take it all in herself. “First Mr. Sexy. Now Mr. Fox. You’re on one heck of a roll.” She runs her hands up and down my back.

“What in the heck are you doing?” I buck her off like a reflex as three officers turn their heads this way for a moment.

“I’m trying to get your luck to rub off on me.”

Noah comes back. His presence suddenly feels larger

than life, and I can't help but note how that baby blue dress shirt sets off his eyes and a tiny part of me hates myself for it.

"Any news?" I say as if the events of the day could somehow shift into something positive.

His lips purse as he takes in a deep breath. "There is. They've got a lead on who a suspect might be."

"Great! Who is it?"

His chest expands a moment, and I try not to notice how wide and steely it looks from this vantage point. "It's you, Lottie. You're the number one suspect." His gaze stays trained on mine a moment too long before he heads back to the crime scene.

"Oh, Lottie"—Keelie wraps her arms around me tight—"it's going to be all right. Just you wait and see."

"Not for Merilee it won't." A flicker of something orange catches my eye at the base of the orchard, and I watch as the outline of a cat slowly fills in. It's that orange tabby that hovered around Merilee this morning making another appearance, and my eyes widen.

My word, this has been the worst thing that has ever happened to anyone before as far as those peculiar phantasms are concerned. And to think I had hoped to see her fall down those courthouse stairs.

No, this is far worse than a skinned knee.

Someone killed Merilee Simonson, and I'm the number one suspect.

CHAPTER 5

There are a few basic principles of baking that every baker worth his or her salt understands without question. First and foremost, if you're following a recipe, you should always read it through to the end before you so much as lift a finger in the kitchen. Just about every other baking catastrophe could be linked to the fact a baker has decided to eschew that little sheet of instructions. Second, set out ingredients and any bowls, measuring cups, and spoons in advance to cut down the time it might take to hunt them down. It's also a saving grace to know well beforehand if you're missing a vital ingredient. Sure, you can substitute your way around an ingredient or two, but it's no fun to run out of flour just as you're about to whip up a last-minute batch of chocolate chip cookies. Third, you might want to clean up as you go. It can quickly get hectic amidst the chaos of dirty mixing bowls, errant spills, and a film of flour lining the counters and the floors. Baking should be a relaxing experience, never a bother.

It's nearly afternoon, almost twenty-four hours after Merilee was found dead on the Grands' property, and I'm trying to get my heart into baking a dozen pumpkin rolls for the diner.

My mother and sister showed up a few minutes ago and have stood on the other end of my workspace with their mouths agape as I recount the gruesome details.

"How could you not pick up the phone and call me?" Lainey looks as if I just knifed up half the town. Her face is paler than the flour I'm using, and her eyes are as wide as eggs. Lainey and I might not be blood-related, but there is a similar look we share, both with wavy caramel-colored hair, large, hazel-green eyes. I suppose those are common traits in general, but I like the way they loosely link me that much more to her as a sister. Meg, our other sister, the one in Vegas, dyes her natural honeyed locks jet black and wears bright yellow contacts when she performs. She's a bit larger than life both on and off the female wrestling circuit.

Mom steps up while burying her fists firmly into her hips. "How could you not call *me*? I'm the mother! I'm supposed to be aware of everything you girls do! I'm a failure at life if I don't know that my sweet baby girl has just been accused of murder. And murder? Really, Lottie? You could have just moved out and avoided this entire nightmare."

I can't help but avert my eyes at my mother's logic. "I didn't murder anybody." The words come from me alarmingly calmer than expected. "And I'm sorry I didn't call either of you. I went straight home and fell asleep with Pancake on my lap. As soon as the sun rose, I took a shower and made my way here. There's no way I want to have another run-in with Mora Anne. Not after her sister was so brutally murdered."

"Stabbed to death seven times!" Lainey clutches at her throat. "Tanner says that's indicative of a crime of passion."

I can't help but frown, and not because of Merilee or any crime of passion. Tanner is Lainey's current boyfriend who I'm still convinced isn't the real deal. Everyone knows that Forest Donovan is the love of her life. But they had some ridiculous falling-out last summer at the infamous county fair, and they've been avoiding one another ever since. Tanner is nothing but a ploy to make Forest jealous. I don't care how much Lainey refuses to admit it. Anyone with eyes can see it.

Lainey shakes her head. "Merilee must have gotten someone really riled up to go after her like that. Although, I pointed out to him that Merilee and the word *passion* were sort of an oxymoron. I can't imagine there's a person on the planet who could muster up enough passionate rage against her."

"Agree," I say weakly. I can't help but make a face as I put the batter for the pumpkin rolls into the oven. The entire kitchen smells of cinnamon and spices. Usually baking this roll, taking in these heavenly scents, would put me in a great mood and make me swoon. Fall is one of my favorite seasons for the baking that comes with it alone, but not today. There is no great mood or swooning. "Poor Mora. I can't imagine what she might be going through."

"Speaking of the Simonson sisters"—Mom swoops in and rubs my back—"how did the hearing go yesterday? I suppose it's a moot point now after everything that's happened."

"No, actually, it's not. But it ended in my favor." I take in my sweet mother with her cranberry lipstick and matching cranberry pea coat. Her hair is dyed a buttery blonde and has been for as long as I can remember. My mother has had a habit of looking impeccably put together, and come hell or high homicide, she still manages to pull it off.

"*Homicide.*" I steady myself against the steel table in the kitchen. "I can't believe there's a *killer* on the loose out there who actually managed to *kill* poor Merilee, and so violently at that."

Lainey gives a frantic nod. "The worst part about all of this is that they think it was you!"

"You are not helping," I'm quick to inform my sister before pulling out the ingredients for the cranberry carrot cake I'm about to bake next. "And you both do realize I'm innocent, right?" I offer up a hardened stare their way until they both nod in unison.

"Of course, honey." Mom is back to giving my back a light massage. "Captain Turner doesn't think you're even mildly responsible. I spoke with Becca this morning, and she assured me of it." Becca is Keelie's mother, Captain Jack Turner's ex-wife, and for the sake of mild sense of loyalty, my mother has kept all of her correspondence with the captain to be relegated through his wife. Becca and my mother have been good friends for years.

"As he should. I'm *not* mildly responsible. It's a waste of time for them to have me on the suspect list at all. Meanwhile, the real killer is free to flee the country. I bet they've already crossed the Canadian border."

"Who do you think did it?" Lainey snatches an iced pumpkin cookie off a cooling tray. I may have iced them a little too soon, leaving the icing to melt over the tops and run down the sides, but I will admit, they look delicious that way.

"I don't know." My mind reels at the possibilities. "A tourist maybe?"

"Who did you see at the crime scene?" Lainey leans in as if grilling me. "You were the one who found the body. Who did you see in the area?"

That stroll I took through the orchard comes back to me. I had my head in the clouds thinking about *men* of all things. I have never had any luck with the opposite gender, and if yesterday's catastrophe signifies anything at all, I might as well steer clear of them for the rest of my days.

"I don't know"—that scene I came upon after my arrival comes back to me—"wait a minute. I did see something. When I got to the orchard, one of the first things I saw was the Simonson sisters having it out with Eve Hollister and Chrissy Nash."

Mom is quick to wave off the idea that they might be involved with something so sinister. "Eve just had her entire house redone, and it's falling to pieces. Sure, she's angry enough to kill, but, believe me, it wouldn't be Merilee Simonson."

"What about Chrissy?" I abandon my post, behind the counter a moment, and make my way over. Do you think Chrissy is still upset over those rumors of a mystery woman breaking up her marriage?"

Lainey bucks as she leans into our mother as well. "I thought you said Chrissy knew who the other woman was, but Mayor Nash gave her a fist full of dollars to keep it quiet. Was it Merilee?" Lainey looks as if she might be sick.

"No." Mom bats the air between us. "Heavens no. Not Merilee. That woman could peel the paint off a wall with just one look. She was that mean." She shudders. "Forgive me for speaking ill of the dead, but I assure you that Merilee was not Mayor Nash's paramour." She wipes the lint off her sleeve before kissing both Lainey and me on the cheek. "Now I have to go. I'm having lunch with Becca and Nell at Evergreen Manor." She gives a cheeky wink. "Nothing like checking out the competition. Ta-ta!" she sings, waving over her shoulder as she disappears into the Honey Pot.

Lainey wastes no time in leaning in close. Her heavily penciled in brows crouch together in a cartoonish way, and yet she looks as adorable as ever. "Now tell me what really happened. Tanner said something about you having a boyfriend! That sounds like vital information I should have gotten from *you,* by the way." Tanner is the Director of Parks and Recs here in Honey Hollow, and he and his crew always seem to have their nose in everything. "So? Who is he? Spill!"

And I do. I spill everything from Mr. Sexy to Mr. Fox all over again, the unrated version, and Lainey's jaw is suddenly rooted to the floor.

"Oh my shooting stars! You are a bonafide sex kitten!"

"Would you stop?" I swat her with a dishtowel. "I'm no such thing. I have lousy luck with men, and you know it. And come to find out, I have even lousier luck with landlords. One of them is dead, and the other is holding fast to the eviction. But, to be perfectly honest, I think I'd be loading up my Honda anyway after yesterday's murderous turn of events. Know of any cheap places that might take a homicide suspect and a finicky Himalayan?" I raise a brow at my suggestive sister.

Her mouth rounds out with delight. "You can live with me!"

"With you?" My entire body bucks at the prospect. I love my sister dearly, and I also love our relationship dearly, but we both know growing up together was no picnic. I like to tease that we never spoke a civil word until I got back from New York. Only it's not a joke. It's one hundred percent true. "You do realize this is me you're speaking with. You know we'd make lousy roommates. That's why we didn't shack up together to begin with. You used to flush my makeup sponges down the toilet!"

"Because you wore my sweaters without asking!" She comes at me with just enough venom.

"You took scissors to my favorite T-shirt!" I can't help but raise my voice an octave.

"Because you threatened to make copies of my diary and pass them out to everyone in your fourth period English class!" she shouts back.

"It was a lesson on bad grammar, and I needed to bring in writing samples!" I cry, and no sooner do I get the last word out than we both break out into laughter.

Lainey wipes the tears from her eyes as she struggles to settle down. "We're not really going to kill each other, are we?"

"I'd be careful if I were you. I am the lead suspect in an active homicide investigation."

"Duly noted." She cinches her purse over her shoulder and gives me a quick embrace. "I'll hide the kitchen knives."

"You're not funny," I say as she heads toward the back door.

"I'll pick up some great books from the library for us, and we can snuggle by the fire and read just like we used to."

"Sounds good!" I call after her. "Get a couple for Pancake, too! He happens to be an avid connoisseur of books!" It just so happens to be his favorite thing to nibble on when I'm not home. I'm sure that furry feline has chewed, licked, and turned his nose up at just about everything he can get his paws on when I'm not around.

That ghostly cat of Merilee's comes back to my mind. I still can't get over what a violent omen that turned out to be. I'd give anything to not see another dead pet or human, in their ghostly form or not.

Merilee might be dead, but something tells me this entire nightmare is far from over.

CHAPTER 6

The Honey Pot not only guarantees a five-star dining experience—a bit of a surprise for what it is—but it also guarantees a great photo op. In fact, the Honey Pot Diner was voted Vermont's most photographed restaurant last year in some hokey poll on the internet. Years ago, when Nell and her husband opened this place, she wanted something to set it apart from what used to be a competing restaurant across the street, so she had an oversized fireplace built against the north wall and a large resin tree planted right in the middle of the restaurant. The tree itself is modeled after the spreading oaks Nell said she used to swing from as a child, and each of the dozens of branches extend to the far corners of the ceiling. It wasn't until about twenty years ago that Nell finally had the idea to wrap each of the individual branches with twinkle lights. That little detail alone has made the Honey Pot what the locals call the most romantic restaurant in the state. We keep them lit during daylight hours too, and even though the effect isn't nearly as dramatic, it's stunning nonetheless. The trunk of the tree is hollowed out and inside sits a honey pot with what looks to be honey dripping down the sides. That right there is what cemented this place as a Honey Hollow treasure. We're practically a landmark at this point, and, according to the tourists who keep this place hopping on its toes, we are just that.

I've finished my baking duties for the day, and just as I'm about to head home and start on the arduous task of packing, I spot a familiar dark-headed man seated at a booth perusing a menu as if he were just some ordinary customer.

"Is that really..." I suck in a quick breath as he turns his stubble-peppered face my way, and I choke on my next thought. "What in the heck?" I head on over just as Keelie waves to me from across the restaurant and points his way. I'm quick to avert my eyes. Keelie is in love with the idea of love. She is obsessed with men. But as fate would have it, she's had just as much luck with them as I have.

"Excuse me?" I no sooner arrive at his table than I set

my feet in a defiant stance. There's only so much disruption I can take in my life, and I hit my limit the second I spotted Merilee's face buried in one of my cutie pies. "Judge Everett Baxter?"

He glances up and does an immediate double take. "Keep your distance," he teases with a sardonic look on his face. "I'd hate for us to inadvertently wrestle it out in such a nice establishment." He looks back to his menu as if I were suddenly invisible.

"Very funny. You are a riot. What are you doing here?" My voice is laced with malice, and I can't help it. It was that unfortunate run-in, and I mean that in the physical sense, that kick-started an entire chain of unfortunate events that followed.

"What are *you* doing here?" He pauses a moment as if reflecting on something. "That's right, this is your neck of the woods, isn't it? The Simonson sisters' shop is in Honey Hollow." He glares at the window as if he sees that Busy Bee of a malfeasance.

"So, do you know?" Suddenly I'm a lot less ticked and a lot more curious. "About Merilee?" I whisper. "You know she's dead, right?" I practically mouth the words.

"What?" His head inches back a notch, and it's only then I note he's dressed to impress in a three-piece suit, a silver tie that dips down to his nether regions like a spear, and something in me heats at the prospect. "What do you mean she's dead?"

"She's dead. Dead as a doornail. Met her maker. Is about to take one long dirt nap."

He frowns a moment, and his eyebrows dance like dark caterpillars framing his handsome face. "You're kidding, right?" he flatlines. "After all, it was you who told me you wanted to wring her neck. For your sake, Ms. Lemon, I hope you're speaking in metaphors."

"What's this?" a decidedly male voice pipes up from behind, and I turn around to find another tall, dark, and equally handsome man—sans the three-piece suit, but equally obnoxious nonetheless.

I stand up straight at the sight of him. "Well, if it isn't my new boyfriend, Noah Private Eye Fox. What do you want?" I snipe just as enthusiastically as I did with Everett.

Everett bucks and coughs as if he had suddenly inhaled hard candy. "You're seeing this woman?"

I suck in a quick breath as I look to the surly judge. "You know this man?"

Everett and Noah exchange steely glares, and suddenly it feels as if a volatile situation is about to erupt.

"Yeah," Noah says it just above a whisper. "He knows me." His scathing gaze remains for a moment more before he looks to me and softens. "I'll stop by some other time." He takes off toward the door just as a bubbly redhead makes her way over with a deep, husky laugh already working its way up her throat. I recognize that bombastic bombshell as none other than Collette Jenner. She's a few years older than me, and if I'm not mistaken, she graduated with Lainey.

"Essex!" She lets out a riotous cackle, garnering the attention of every unfortunate soul in the room. "How I love to say your name." He stands as she lunges over him with a hearty embrace, and I take that as my cue. I don't stick around for the Essex-Collette Hour. Instead, I make a beeline outside and catch the faint shadow of Noah Fox as he makes his way toward his office.

"Noah!" I call out, and a plume of fog bursts from me, pale as a paper lantern into the moonless night.

He turns around and lifts an arm.

"Did you stop in to see me?" My heart riots against my chest as my adrenaline kick-starts for seemingly no reason.

"I did," he calls back, and his teeth glow a moment as if he were smiling. "I'll stop by another time."

"Sounds good!" My entire body turns into one giant heartbeat, and for the life of me I can't figure out why. It sure as heck isn't because of some real or imagined boyfriend.

I'm not really looking forward to meeting up with Noah again, am I?

A part of me already knows the answer to that.

To quote Keelie—"Lottie Lemon, I never knew you."

CHAPTER 7

There's a lot to be said for moving, and not one word of it is good.

I hold Pancake tight as we survey the damage. Wobbly boxes form towers taller than me by the entry, and bags and bags of trash sit slumped over in the corner, ready to be chucked into the nearest dumpster. And, of course, let's not forget the discards ready to go back to the secondhand store from whence they came—old sweaters that have grown too tight and jeans that won't make it past my thighs. They say you should never trust a skinny baker, and judging by the speed my curves are filling in nicely, you would think I had set out to be the most trustworthy baker in the world.

"What do you think?" I press a kiss over the top of Pancake's soft forehead, and he looks up at me with those glowing gray eyes before letting out a weak *rawrrr*. He's always been good at holding a conversation. At least he seems to be when he answers at the appropriate intervals. Lord knows I've carried on one gab session too many with this fabulous feline, and I swear on all the water in Honey Lake that Pancake is not only cheaper than therapy but far more effective. And that's not some loose guess. There was some actual high-priced therapy involved after the New York debacle, while I was still in New York. Lucky for me, my therapist let me pay in Bundt cakes. It turns out, she had a mad hankering for the marbled Bundt cake that her mother used to make as a child. So while I worked out my mommy issues, she indulged in hers as well.

A knock erupts on the door, and I glance through the peephole in the event it's Mora Anne who, ironically, I've grown to be deathly afraid of in a span of less than forty-eight hours. But it's not Mora. It's a face I don't even recognize. A tall, dark-haired woman who looks like she could be Merilee if Merilee actually smiled and had a mild flirtation of joy in her eye.

I hope to high heaven this isn't the new and improved post-mortem version of Merilee. The last thing I need is another fantastic phantasm in my life. Not that there was anything particularly fantastic about Merilee in general, and that's not a quip. It's merely a fact.

Have I mentioned that I'm beyond tired and cranky? My sanity came apart ten times while cleaning out my bathroom. How in the world did I end up with three trash bags full of things I absolutely cannot part with? Lainey is right. I am a hoarder. A horrible hoarder at that because I haven't even amassed that much junk yet. But now that I'm living with Lainey for the foreseeable future, I might just splurge and make up for lost crap.

I swing the door open, and my stomach drops at the sight of her. There is something decidedly Simonson about her, it's haunting.

"Can I help you?"

She's dressed head to toe in a navy velour duster with blanked silver buttons running along the length of it, and this seemingly Simonson detail alarms me.

"Just looking to see what I'm up against." She plucks off her black fitted gloves as she strides past me. Her eyes never once meet with me. It's as if I were invisible, or the help. "Lowered ceilings in the hall?" She gags on sight as she does a quick loop through the small space before her. "I'll obviously have to downsize." She nods to the fireplace. "How quaint. I'm used to bigger, of course. My fireplace back in Connecticut could roast a deer." Her head lolls lazily in my direction. "I'll need you out by noon. My movers are paid by the hour, and I'm not looking to part with my inheritance so early."

Inheritance? That about says it all.

"Well, um, hello. I'm Lottie Lemon." I squeeze Pancake to me as if protecting him from the onslaught. Usually I would introduce Pancake as well, but something tells me this Simonson knockoff wouldn't appreciate the energy spent to do so. And for the record, anyone who doesn't appreciate Pancake doesn't appreciate me.

I hold my hand out between us, and she stares at it as if it were a novelty I was showing off.

"Cascade Montgomery—relation to Mora and the late Merilee." She twists her lips as if she didn't morally approve of Merilee's passing.

"Cascade?" *Like the dishwashing detergent,* I'm tempted to ask, but I value Pancake's life, and something tells me she's not above swinging a tail or two if she gets thrown in a tizzy.

"Yes"—she takes a menacing step in—"is there something you find offensive about my name?"

Real world translation: *you got a problem with that?*

It's quickly becoming evident Cascade isn't from anywhere near the real world. I'll bet every last wobbly box in this place that the mother ship dropped her off.

"I think you have a lovely name. But the fact is, there's only an hour left to meet your deadline, and my best friend hasn't even shown up with the sweet treat and coffee she swore up and down she was scouting all of Honey Hollow for. I've still got a bedframe to dismantle and a bookshelf that will need to be tied twelve ways to Sunday on top of my poor Honda, not to mention the mattress, sofa, and dresser—all of which I pray can fit into my sister's garage.

Have you seen the prices they want at these storage facilities? Highway robbery at knifepoint would be more painless." No sooner do I make the violent analogy than a visual of Merilee lying in a pool of her own blood flits through my mind. "I apologize. That was terribly insensitive of me. I'm so sorry for your loss. I'm sure your entire family misses her deeply."

She sniffs at the thought. "They're all dead now, except for Mora." She averts her eyes as if that were the real tragedy brewing. And, sadly, for the two of them, it might be. I doubt either Mora Anne or Cascade here gets along with anyone, let alone each other.

"So you see"—I quickly change the subject as I motion to the carnage around me—"I can't possibly be out in an—"

The door bursts open and in spills Keelie with two cups of coffee and a grinning Noah Corbin Fox on her tail. "I've got coffee and one big sweet treat for you just like I promised." She bumps her hip to his, and he keeps on grinning my way as if he knew a secret. I bet he knows just how much it annoys me to see him. "Noah brought his truck, so you'll be out in an hour!" She buzzes past me, and a breath hitches in my throat as I'm about to say something.

Noah Fox looks alarmingly comely in his orange and black flannel, his dark inky jeans, and worn looking leather work boots. Men in uniform hypnotize some women, but it's always been men in flannel who have taken my breath away—sort of the way Noah Fox is doing now.

I turn back to Cascade and manufacture a quick smile. "I'll be out in an hour."

It takes exactly that long for us to fill both my car and Keelie's, not to mention Noah's truck. Lainey had to work this morning or she would have gladly been here, too. For a fleeting moment this morning, I had considered calling Bear and breaking my vow of questionable silence in exchange for some transportation capabilities his flatbed would have been able to afford me, but it turns out, Noah's shiny new ride is far roomier.

"Well done," I pant as I take in the miracle he's managed in the back of his truck. He's layered my mattress, box spring, bookcase, sofa, and even tucked my coffee table in the back of the puzzle-like lair. "I think you're ready to level up in Tetris." I hold up Pancake and wave at Noah with his paw as if he were agreeing with me.

"That I am." He laughs while leaning in, touching his nose to Pancake's. "I think your mom is officially delirious. She's actually spoken a kind word to me."

"You got the delirious part right."

His hair catches the light, and under those chocolate brown waves there's a hint of fire in them, and it only intrigues me more. Who knew I'd be so shallow as to be entranced by hair of all things? Okay, so it's not just the hair but the biceps I've watched bounce for the better half of the last hour, the way his tongue slips to the side of his mouth when he's in deep concentration, and the way he looked morbidly determined while dismantling my bedframe. I especially liked how kind he was while pretending not to see the bevy of wadded up panties under my bed. I swear, while I'm changing into my PJ's, laundry is the last thing on my mind, but I blamed the whole thing on Pancake just to be safe.

"You know you didn't have to do this." It comes out soft, less abrasive than anything I've said to him before.

Keelie pops up with her bandana slipping into her eyes, her blonde curls twirling every which way. "That's what boyfriends do, hon. They help you move." She takes an earnest swig from her coffee. "That's what took me so long in getting here. I had to search high and low before I could chase this fox out of his hole." She leans in with a devilish look in her eye. "He lives in the housing tract just above the Evergreen Manor. Second house at the end of Country Cottage Road."

My stomach sours when she mentions the Evergreen Manor. That means his house is just a hop and a skip away from Naomi's stomping grounds. I'm sure just one look at Noah and she'll have her claws sunk a shade too close to his family jewels. Naomi is infamous for grabbing men by the collar and stealing them away. She's beautiful—as is her twin standing in front of me—most men don't put up much of a fight.

"I wanted to," Noah adds. "You helped me out the other day. It was the least I could do to return the favor."

"Yes, well, your favor far outweighs mine by a three quarter-ton mile." I give the side of his truck a quick pat. "There has to be some way I can repay you."

His brow lifts, and he doesn't miss a beat. "There is."

Keelie hops behind him and puckers her lips suggestively before snatching Pancake from me and heading to her car.

Noah rests his arm along the side of his truck and leans in, boxing me in, and it feels warm, intimate. "I'm heading over to the orchard tomorrow to take another look at the scene of the crime. Join me."

My mouth falls open as I inspect him in this close proximity. Of all the men I've dated, this unofficial boyfriend of mine takes the cake for most handsome and simultaneously irritating on some strange, primal level.

"I'll be at the orchard tomorrow afternoon. I have to pick apples for the pies I'll be baking."

"Good." His eyes squint out a smile all their own. "It looks like we're going apple picking."

"I guess we are."

Noah helps offload everything into Lainey's garage and takes off while Keelie and I watch his truck drive out of sight.

She sinks her elbow into my rib. "I guess you really do have a boyfriend."

"*Please*. I hardly know the guy, Keelie. He could still very well be the murderer."

"You'll get to know him plenty tomorrow. I heard that whole *let's load up on some apples while we load up on each other* spiel. Open up to this one, would you? Maybe this time it won't end up biting you in the behind."

I look to the empty road in front of us as the dust settles from his wake.

"Lately everything has been biting me in the behind. I don't know why this would be any different."

And then something Cascade said hits me from left field, and my mouth falls open.

I think I just solved a very murderous mystery.

CHAPTER 8

Cider Grove Orchards gleams like a jewel under the autumn sun. The fields are golden, and the verdant trees are loaded with amber, green, and ruby red apples. There's a chill in the air that holds the light scent of cinnamon and spices as we pass the cider press. The ground is peppered with maroon maple leaves that stamp against the hillside like hands. And the birch trees rise high into the sky around the periphery, shimmering golden in the crisp breeze.

"It's beautiful here." Noah scoops a basket out of the reserve as we head deep into the orchard, and I lead us toward a bumper crop of Pippins, Pink Ladies, and Honeycrisps.

"It is beautiful," I say, tossing a Pink Lady into his basket. "That's why I never want to leave again. Honey Hollow is home. There's not another living soul I'd give the power to chase me out of here again."

"Again?" He tips his head my way, amused. Noah has a charm about him, something disarming that makes you trust him far too soon. Maybe he is cut out for the PI business after all. "Ah, yes. New York. I thought you went for school?"

"I did, but I stayed for me, or so I thought. I never really belonged there, but a part of me never wanted to come back."

He drops the basket between us and begins plucking the rose-colored apples clean from nearby limbs. "So what, or should I say who, chased you out?"

I give a wry smile as I toss an apple to him and he catches it close to his chest.

"You first. What happened in Cincinnati? Let me guess, you're wanted in Ohio?"

He barks out a short-lived laugh. "Believe me, I'm not wanted in Ohio. I'm not sure I'm wanted anywhere at this point."

"Is that where you're originally from? Ohio?" I'm still curious how he seemed to know Everett. But then, Everett is a judge, and Noah is in a quasi-law enforcement field himself.

"Nope." He tosses in another several apples, and our basket is already filled a good foot. "Vermont born and raised. Grew up in Hollyhock, moved to Fallbrook when I was in high school." His features harden. Whatever happened in Fallbrook wasn't a good thing.

"Wow, we were practically neighbors." I toss another pink apple his way. This time far softer, more as a peace offering than a taunt. "So, did you move to Cincinnati for work? Or love?" A handsome man like Noah couldn't possibly stay single for long. And that pained look in his eyes when he spoke of no one wanting him in Ohio was a glaring arrow toward a broken heart. A part of me hurts for him. I know that pain, and I wouldn't wish that kind of agony on my worst enemy.

Noah blows a breath through his cheeks as we pick up the basket and move to the next tree over. "Both I guess. Honestly, it was just for love. I had a pretty great job in Vermont. Had a great one in Ohio until I didn't."

"Did they let you go?" I head over to a stepladder and hike up on the first rung before reaching for the highest fruit I can.

"If let go is the same as being fired, then yes."

I turn my full attention to him once again and suck in a quick breath. "You were *fired*?" My mouth falls open with a smile.

"Does this please you in some twisted way?" His brows do a little dance before narrowing into a V, and something deep inside of me wholeheartedly approves of that vexingly handsome look.

"Only because you seem so perfect." Now it's me scowling at him. "But I'm sorry to hear it. Can I ask—what in the world did you do to deserve the chopping block?"

Noah purses his lips as he looks to the east, and the sunlight cuts through his eyes making them glow like emeralds on fire.

It occurs to me that Noah might not be up for sharing—that he might not have ever shared the dark circumstances that surround his time in Cincinnati. Whatever happened there was bad. I already know that.

"It's okay"— I reach out and brush my fingers against his chest—"you don't need to go there."

"No, it's fine. Really." He squints into the sun a moment, and I can't help but note that standing on this first rung puts us eye to eye. My gaze dips to his mouth a moment, and I admire how perfectly formed his lips are. "I was a homicide detective on the force. Found my wife with another man and my temper got away from me one night. I shot out the back tires of his car with my weapon, and that was that. Had my badge suspended indefinitely."

"Oh, wow." My heart thumps wild at the visual. Noah doesn't strike me as the angry type, but under those circumstances, who could blame him? "I'm sorry to hear it. That must have been very hard for you."

"Getting fired? Yes, it was." He slaps the back of his neck and gives it a scratch. "The breakup was a little tough, too. Didn't see it coming."

I let go of a breath I didn't know I was holding. "I didn't either." The words string from my lips before I can stop them. It was never my intention to say it. I have no plans on extrapolating on what went on in New York. There are some wounds that feel raw long after they should have healed. Mine was one of them, and judging by that look in Noah's eyes, so was his.

He takes up my hand and pulls me to him by my fingers. His eyes stay trained on mine, sincere and serious. "I'm sorry to hear that, Lottie. I would never want you to feel that."

"It wasn't fun."

The two of us sway toward one another, and my eyes expand as he comes in close. Noah Fox has a way about him that is larger than life. For sure he's far too handsome for me to comprehend that he's standing here with me on purpose. There is not a planet in the solar system in which I would think a man like Noah would be interested in someone like me.

A blustery wind picks up and sends me toppling onto his chest, and I freeze. Noah's lips flicker with the faintest smile, and he ever so carefully bows his head toward mine.

We're going to do it. It's going to happen. Noah Fox is going to go for the gold and is about to grace my lips with his. I'm pretty sure I'm not going to stop him. What's a simple kiss going to hurt? But I think we both know there's nothing simple about a kiss.

A small crowd moves in and starts to liven up the vicinity, filling it thick with bodies.

I pull back as Noah and I share an uneasy glance.

"We should finish up—" I shrug.

"With the apples." A slight dimple goes off in his left cheek, and my insides dissolve at the sight of it. So not fair.

Noah and I fill that basket to the brim and each grab a handle to take back to the barn.

"Hey, Holland," I say, breathless as we come upon my old friend. "Got a bushel of apples ready to go. How much do I owe?"

Holland cuts his hand through the air. "You just keep turning those apples into caramel gold. Those pies were a hit with both the staff and family."

"Thank you. I appreciate that." I take a step toward the counter. Holland is a tall man with red curly hair and perpetually tanned skin. He's a sweetheart and easy on the eyes. It's exactly why Meg fell so hard for him.

"Sorry about Merilee." He shakes his head while looking from me to Noah. "But it wasn't your pie that killed her. Your pies are welcome at the Apple Festival, and I have no doubt they're going to be a big hit."

I glance to Noah for a moment, and he gives a subtle nod.

"Say"—I start slow—"you wouldn't happen to know what Merilee was doing here that afternoon, would you?" I seem to vaguely recall something about a craft booth, but there's a murderer on the loose and I'm hoping Holland might know something.

He tips his head back a moment while tossing his gaze

in the direction of the spot we found Merilee. Correction —I found Merilee.

"She and Mora swung by to speak with my sister, Tara."

"About a booth for the festival?" As soon as I give him the out, I regret it. There's a look in his eyes that suggests it was a little more complicated than that.

"No, they've already paid their table fee." He looks to Noah. "Tara's an attorney. They said they wanted legal advice."

"Legal advice? We had gone to court that morning. They lost the verdict. The judge said they didn't have a case. I can't imagine what they could have wanted to discuss with her."

Holland shakes his head. "I can't answer that. Tara's in Ashford today. I can tell her to give you a call if you want."

"I'd appreciate that."

Holland picks up the apples. "Is that your truck out there?" he calls out to Noah as he makes his way toward the parking lot.

"Sure is," Noah shouts back, and soon enough Holland is out the door and setting them in the back of Noah's flatbed.

Noah and I make our way to the side of the barn to the exact place where Merilee Simonson met her demise and gaze down at the earth covered with leaves and a small floral arrangement of mums and asters. It feels solemn, holy.

Noah places his hand over my shoulder and leans in. "What kind of legal advice do you think they were after?"

Their odd cousin, Cascade, comes to mind, and I relay it to Noah as best as I can recall. "She said all of her relatives were dead except for Mora. Cascade is the reason I was being evicted to begin with."

"Do you know what she's doing in town?"

"No clue."

His face smooths out, and I can see the kernel of an idea brewing in his eyes. "Then that's exactly what we need to find out."

CHAPTER 9

In general, it's a rare occasion for Lainey and me to have a day off in common. It's more than a rare event for us to be experiencing it together while waking up under the same roof.

I finish up in the kitchen with the crepes and bring them out to my sister who is currently wrapped up in a blanket staring vacantly at her laptop. Pancake is curled up behind her, having already made the top of the sofa his favorite little perch. The feisty feline opens an eye lazily as I take a seat next to my sister.

"I come bearing gifts." I set down the tray of chocolate hazelnut crepes and steaming hot lattes onto the coffee table. A slathering of hazelnut crème lands on my finger, and I indulge in licking it right back off. "*Mmm,* so delicious. You're welcome, by the way." I give her foot a light tap with my own.

"Oh, sorry." She comes to long enough to observe the goodies before us. "Hey, thank you! I thought you had something delicious going on in there."

"Don't you ever doubt me." I spot a familiar pine tree logo gleaming with pride on her laptop screen and grunt in its direction. "Is that what you can't turn your head away from?"

"That's right." She gives a wistful shake of the head while pulling her laptop between us. "The Evergreen Manor is hosting a charity auction this Friday night to help offset Merilee's funeral expenses. Apparently, the sisters really hit hard times."

"Geez"—I say, taking the laptop from her so I can get a better look—"I knew they were having a tough time, but I had no idea it was that bad."

"Funerals generally cost an arm and a leg—and not the dead kind. They want a pound of living, breathing flesh to pay for that good time. It looks like all of the local businesses have pitched in a freebie of some sort to auction off. Look here"—she points to the screen—"the Honey Pot is offering a one hundred dollar gift card."

"I see. Wow, that's very generous of Nell. That woman has a bigger heart than anyone I know."

"So, are you going?" Lainey is both grinning like a loon and has that *I'm terrified for you* look on her face. It's a quizzical feat that only Lainey seems able to pull off.

"I'd like to. They say the killer always goes back to the scene of the crime—which I did yesterday, by the way. And I'm sure having me at the auction would be just as disrespectful."

"Who says that?"

"I don't know—TV shows." I bat that judgmental look on her face away. "But I think I'd like to go. Besides, it would be interesting to see who'd come out."

"Everyone's going as far as I can tell. The Simonson sisters may not have been very friendly, but they're one of our own. And if Honey Hollow prides itself on anything, it's taking care of one of our own."

"Duly noted."

"And did you see this?" She points to the fine print. "The Honey Pot will be providing complimentary appetizers and delectable desserts. That's you, my sweet sister. It looks like you'll be there one way or another."

"Huh. I guess I will. What does one bake for a funeral fundraiser?"

"Cookies in the shape of caskets?"

"Lainey!" I can't help but give a sorrowful chuckle. I know for a fact she's teasing. Lainey and I have always dealt with the tough stuff through humor. I don't see that changing anytime soon. "How about cookies in the shape of pumpkins? Or better yet—autumn leaves? That's respectable. I can ice them in red, orange, and yellow. That way, it will truly look like fall in Honey Hollow. It's both tasteful *and* seasonal."

"I think it's a great idea. So, are you bringing a date?" Her shoulders dance up and down as she purrs with glee.

"A *date*? What? No. It's a somber occasion. It's not a dance or a formal event." I can't help but wrinkle my nose at my sister. "I take it you're bringing Tanner. You two seem inseparable lately. Please tell me this isn't the real thing." I pull forward a chocolate hazelnut crepe and moan my way through the first, rich, creamy bite. It tastes like a cloud dipped in heaven.

Lainey lifts a shoulder at the thought of her fake love. I don't care how much time they decide to waste together. My loyalty lies with Forest. That boy loved her, and she loved him. I've never seen a fiercer brand of affection. Not even what I had in New York could compare.

"I don't know," she bleats it out while tossing her hands in the air. "At first, I thought this might be fun, and then before I knew it, we were doing couple things—the movies, double dates, taking hikes around the hillsides. And then two weeks ago, we went to his cousin's wedding in Leeds, and I met every last member of his family. It just felt so very official." Lainey's face loses color, and my heart breaks for her. "And you know?" She shakes her head while gazing at some unknowable horizon. "I kind of like it. I like the idea of a normal relationship. Not once have we gotten into a spat. Not once have we disagreed on anything. He's kind and gentle and—"

"Boring as oatmeal." I don't mind finishing the sentiment for her at all. "So, are the two of you, you know"—I wiggle my shoulders at her—"getting serious in that sense?" I glance to her lap, and she tosses a pillow at me.

Her lips part as she carefully considers her wording. Lainey and I are close. When she lost her virginity to Forest, she was very frank with me. And after I stopped vomiting for a week straight, I began to appreciate the new level of trust our relationship took on.

"Let's just say he's never spent the night."

"Good. Let's keep it that way."

She gives me the side-eye, and suddenly I feel like I'm in for it. "And what's going on with this boyfriend of yours? I'm not sure how I feel about him materializing out of the blue. Who is this Noah Fox guy, and why am I suddenly suspicious of his presence in my sister's life? You do realize that level of innate distrust in a sister means he's the real deal."

"He is not the real deal. And he is certainly not my boyfriend. Not in real life anyway."

She squints over at me until her eyes look like miniature half-moons. "Have you kissed?"

"Almost. But it didn't happen. See? Not real. Totally imagined."

"You almost kissed, and this is the first I'm hearing about it?" She swats me on the arm before shoveling a crepe into her mouth, and no sooner does she groan in appreciation than my cell phone goes off.

"Honey Hollow Savings and Loan." I make a face at the name above the number. I've called a time or two to make sure a check has cleared, but I've never had them call me.

"Hello?" I add a touch of cheer to my voice, far too cheery to be real this early in the morning before putting the phone on speaker. Lainey is going to listen in anyhow. I might as well make it easy for her.

"Hello, Lottie? This is Ellen Rawlings down at the bank. I just wanted to let you know there was a very big deposit added to your checking account this morning."

"There was?" I look to Lainey as my eyes spring wide. "Who made it?" My heart thumps wild inside my chest. I'm the only one who's ever deposited anything into my bank account, and the prospect of someone else doing so mildly alarms me.

"It was a cashier's check. The depositor wishes to remain anonymous, but they did ask us to pass along a message."

"What's that?"

"They said the money was to be used to purchase new appliances."

"Appliances?" I exchange a curious look with my sister, considering the fact I don't have a kitchen to outfit anything new with.

"I'll tell you what"—Ellen gives a dark laugh—"I don't know what kind of a kitchen you have, but this is a large chunk of change. You have more than enough to outfit the Honey Pot with a brand new kitchen if you wanted."

I suck in a breath as the message becomes clear as the autumn breeze drumming against the door.

I hang up with Ellen and hug my sister tight. "Get dressed. We're headed to Main Street."

"To the Honey Pot?"

"Someplace better. The bakery. Someone just gifted me a windfall so I can outfit it with brand new appliances."

"A windfall? Who in their right mind would give you cash?" she shouts with a twinge of excitement in her voice as she rushes to get her shoes on.

"I don't know, but I have an idea."

"Maybe it's a payout because they think you offed Merilee? You're not moonlighting as a hitman, are you?"

"You're awful. And if you're smart, you'll watch your back."

THE SHOP next door to the Honey Pot is cavernous and mostly empty save for an aluminum table and chairs currently occupied by Keelie, Lainey, and me.

"One hundred thousand dollars?" Lainey has been dumbstruck by the dollar amount ever since we ran by the bank to affirm it.

"I can't believe it myself," I say, taking the restaurant equipment catalog from Keelie. As soon as I texted her the info this morning, she said she knew just the thing to bring. It's a great head start, that's for sure. "Who do you think sent it?" I can't but eye my bestie as if she's up to something. Everyone knows she comes from money.

Keelie's mother, Becca, has a brother named William, and they're forever squabbling over who will get Nell's millions once she passes. William is an attorney in Bassett Ville and has already threatened Becca with the fact that any will can be contested. I'm sure glad neither my mother's nor my father's parents had any real money to speak of. I would never want Lainey and Meg to act like that. Not that they would, but they say money changes people. And when a loaded relative dies, the vultures come out of the woodwork. I wouldn't fight for money, not with my sisters, not with anyone. I've always felt a little like the odd man out in the sense that they were blood and I wasn't, even though they have never made me feel that way. When I was six and my mother dropped the bomb on me that someone left me alone as a newborn in the firehouse, I couldn't help but feel like a discard who had done something so terrible my own real mother—whom I don't call my real mother anymore, but my *bio* mother—would leave me on a grimy floor just hoping a kind man would find me before the wolves jumped in. Of course, the wolves wouldn't have found me in the firehouse, but that's not the point. They could have. I had just seen my friend's baby brother the day before my mother broke the news, and the thing that stuck out at me wasn't his ruby red cuteness—he screamed for the entire hour we visited, there was not one cute thing about him—it was the fact he was so vulnerable. He couldn't do a thing for himself except scream at the top of his lungs, and I found that alarming.

Keelie rolls her eyes and slaps my arm right off the table. "You and I both know who sent it. Grammy Nell. Wasn't she the one who told you she wanted a bakery in this town? And wasn't she the one who said she wanted you to be the head baker? She's just outfitting your shop and she wants you to order what you need."

My mouth falls open as Keelie confirms my suspicions. "Knew it. That sneaky ol' beautiful woman just gave me the kick start I need to get a brand new bakery going. Well, girls, it's time to shop for appliances until we drop."

And we do just that. Because the bare bones of a restaurant are already here, the walk-in refrigerator and freezer, stainless steel counters and a three-compartment sink, we pick out the bare bones of appliances this place will need to get going with enough to spare for refrigerated display cases, small wares, the pots and pans, utensils, and every baking accessory you can think of under the sun. And, of course, the pièce de résistance: a beautiful Hobart mixer. Otis comes by and helps measure and plan a layout that will work. Keelie and Lainey help me choose a beautiful shade of butter yellow to paint the walls, and it all feels as if it's coming together magically.

"Wait a minute"—I cringe as I look to the vast potential seating area in the front of the store—"I don't have a dime left for furniture. I'll need a ton of café tables and chairs to outfit this place, and I know just from seeing the tab at the Honey Pot for replacements how much that can be."

Lainey gives the kitchen a sweeping glance as if it had caused the furniture-based malfeasance. "Maybe you can take that pricey industrial mixer off the list. That thing costs more than my car! You can have my stand mixer. That, plus your own, and you'll have two for the kitchen. Oh! And I think I have a handheld electric somewhere in the back of the garage."

I groan without meaning to. Lainey can't make toast. I shouldn't expect her to see how laughable her idea would be. It would be doable, of course, but the batches would be so very small I could never bake enough to outfit those shelves for the customers.

Keelie shrugs with a look of regret on her face. "I'd offer the mixers at the Honey Pot, but the kitchen staff uses them daily."

"No, that's fine. And they're still not the right size. Besides, Margo and Mannford would kill me."

Bear comes up, holding his hammer over his shoulder, those lids of his in a perpetual bedroom eye position. It's not his fault, really. Bear has thick, heavy lids, so he's always had that sleepy-eyed look about him. His hair is mussed slightly, and I'd like to think that's from working hard, but seeing that he showed up here first thing in the morning I'm betting he got out of bed that way. And if rumors of Bear's love life are true, he didn't wake up alone.

"I've got an idea." He winks my way, and instinctively I

want to swat him. In the past, he always started off our lusty dalliances with those famous last words. "Richie Newton owes me a favor, and his family owns the thrift store. They're forever bogged down with discarded furniture they can't sell. Head on over and pick out what you want. They own a chain of stores, so you can head to Hollyhock, Leeds, and Ashford, too. I'll have Richie give me a call when you're done, and I'll pick up the pieces for you."

The air stills in the room a moment as the three of us try to process the scenario.

"I don't know whether to hug you or slug you." Honestly, it sounds both too good to be true and like a natural disaster in the making. "I'm not sure if I'd rather have people suing me because they're suddenly addicted to chocolate chip cookies or because they busted a hip when they fell out of my rickety old furniture."

"That won't happen," Bear chuckles at the thought. "I'll make sure everything is sturdy enough before I set it in this place." He runs his fingers through his thick curls, and Keelie gives a little sigh. She's always had a slight thing for Bear, but as per girl code he's been off-limits. Believe you me, the reason I don't want Keelie dating Bear has nothing to do with the fact he was my first and everything to do with the fact he's a jackass of the highest order. He's not just a player. He wrote the playbook—and has revised it several times to boot.

"Sounds good." Keelie nods furtively at me as if trying to get me to agree. "We can paint them all to match. It won't be as bad as it sounds." She doesn't sound all that convincing.

"She's right." Lainey offers a commiserating smile. "And I think we should paint them in every shade of pastel. That way we'll be celebrating the fact they don't exactly match. Sort of an organized form of chaos."

"Organized chaos," I repeat as I take a deep breath. Slowly, in my mind's eye, this place comes to life before me, with its butter yellow walls, its pastel furniture looking scrumptious as nonpareils, the showcase shelves filled with every delicious sweet treat I have ever wanted to bake, the gleaming kitchen filled with new appliances, the smooth marble counter over the island—okay, so it's stainless steel for now, but my luck is looking up. It can't hurt to be optimistic at this point. A rush of adrenaline surges in me like never before. "This is really happening."

Lainey offers a partial hug. "It's really happening."

Bear heads for the door. "You know what else is happening?" He nods my way. "You and me at the Evergreen Friday night. Save a dance for me, would you?" There's a glimmer of optimism under that sarcastic demeanor, and I can't help but think Bear is still holding out the vestige of hope for the two of us. He ducks out before I can properly school him. Not that I would after that kind offer he made. Maybe Otis Fisher really is a changed man? Not that it matters. You don't get to run around on me and then get to call me your girlfriend again. New York comes to mind. Come to think of it, I seem to attract a certain type of playboy.

I look to Keelie. "They're not going to have a dance at Merilee's fundraiser, are they?"

Keelie tips her head back as her lips pull into a line. "I only know one thing for sure. Naomi is in charge of the event."

"In that case, I hope she opts for a live band."

CHAPTER 10

Naomi Turner did not opt for a live band. Instead, she has Mutton Darren, the general maintenance manager at the Evergreen Manor, streaming rap music from his phone through an obnoxiously loud speaker the size of my Honda.

"You could have warned me that I needed earmuffs!" Keelie shouts to her older twin, older by two minutes, but those one hundred twenty seconds have been lorded over my best friend for as long as I can remember.

"It'll put people in a good mood," Naomi admonishes with that perennial perturbed look on her face. "And a good mood is a giving mood. Mora Anne says she wants a top-of-the-line casket for her sister." She scoffs down at her own sister. Her heels are so high she's towering over the both of us. Keelie has a softer, friendlier look about her, whereas Naomi looks as if she's about to break the arm of everyone in here. Keelie and Naomi are fraternal twins, which I always thought should have been called sororal twins, but nonetheless they look identical enough with their hair notwithstanding. Keelie is a fresh scrubbed, curly headed blonde, but Naomi has opted to dye her fair locks a shocking shade, the color of a raven's wing. And she spends a copious amount of time each day flat ironing her curls. She's a big fan of *Keeping up with the Kardashians,* and it's no coincidence her hair and overall style took an abrupt U-turn once she began watching the show religiously. "I bet you'd give me the coffee can."

"Only because you'd deserve it." Keelie gives a cheeky wink. "And you're wrong about the giving mood. My entire body feels like a beating heart that's about to give out. You'll be chasing people and their potentially deep pockets away with this noise. If you have a heart of your own, you'll have him turn it down and maybe play something softer, something without expletives or the phrase *you better watch your back.*"

I grimace because that happens to be the refrain going off like a gunshot in our ears. To make it worse, it turns out the coroner confirmed the fact that the knife that inflicted the fatal blow was delivered through poor Merilee's back. I've been asking questions to anyone that will listen, just trying to garner a clue as to what happened to Merilee that day. I'm so thirsty for the truth I'd do anything to solve this mystery.

Naomi snarls before heading toward the grand ballroom to deal with the noise, as Keelie so accurately put it. We're still in the foyer of the Evergreen Manor, a stately building that was once a colonial era home to a rich earl who was determined to be a Yankee. It has a haunted mansion appeal if you ask me with its oversized white pillars in the front and aggressive ironwork scrolling around the balcony. Inside, the walls are paneled with mahogany, and the floors are rich with thick emerald carpet, giving the place a cloistered feel. But it's ironically spacious, and it has its mammoth size working for it in every capacity. The entry and lobby are tastefully decorated with garland comprised solely of fall leaves and pumpkins, and there are oversized pots of mustard yellow mums dotting every entry. A double staircase leads up to a plethora of rooms. Outside of the manor there is only Mom's B&B in all of Honey Hollow and Hollyhock. And if both those places are fully booked, you might find a seedy hotel in Leeds with availability next to one of Bear's favorite stripper hangouts. It's not a shocker that the Evergreen Manor and Mom's place are always booked to capacity.

Forest Donovan walks in looking dapper as the day is long with a suit and fresh shaven face. It turns out, this is a quasi-formal event, per Naomi's public invite. Keelie has donned a flashy red dress, and I opted for something more demure—i.e., the only thing my mobile closet could spit out, a blush pink A-line dress that makes my hips look as if they've doubled in size. One of these days I'm going to rectify my disaster of a wardrobe, but I haven't gotten around to it yet.

"Lottie." Forest grins as he lunges in for a quick embrace. "You look great." There's a veil of sadness in his eyes, and I know it has nothing to do with my illusionary expansive hips and everything to do with my sister. "How's Lainey doing?"

I didn't need a road map to solve that mystery.

Just as I'm about to answer, Keelie elbows me and nods to the entry where Lainey comes in wearing a navy velvet dress that makes her look like a princess—and plastered to her side is Tanner Redwood, still wearing his vest from the parks and rec department. Lainey spots us and quickly threads her arm through Tanner's, speeding them off to the grand room. Judging by that crestfallen look on Forest's face, he witnessed the entire event.

"I guess she's doing just fine." He tips his head our way. "Have a great evening, ladies," he says as he heads in their direction.

"That boy isn't giving up," I say to Keelie. "That's a good man. He's fighting for what he believes in, and that happens to be true love with my sister."

"You say true love. Lainey says stalker."

I give her hip a bump with mine. "She does *not* say that.

At least not to me. Lainey knows how much I love them together. In fact—" I pause a moment as Keelie looks to the entry with wide eyes, and before I can turn my head, Naomi joins us just as transfixed as she looks to the entrance as well.

I glance that way just as an all too familiar brick wall of a body strides my way. "Lemon," he says it stoic as if we were about to head into a boardroom to discuss a hostile takeover.

"Judge Baxter," I say with the same lack of enthusiasm.

"Everett, please." He nods to both Keelie and Naomi, both trying to outdo themselves in the drooling department. Everett looks intimidating as usual in a black suit, gold tie, his dark hair slicked back, and those blue eyes siren at us like a warning. Everything about *Everett* looks like a not-so-veiled threat.

"What are you doing here, Everett? Do I need to initiate a restraining order?" I'm only half-teasing.

Naomi gags as if it were her I was looking to slap with a legal restraint. "Naomi Nell Turner." She's quick to shake Everett's hand, caressing her fingers around his wrist while she does it. "I manage the Evergreen Manor and would like to personally welcome you to this fine establishment. Our dining room is always open to the public—the only real five-star restaurant in either Honey Hollow, Hollyhock, or Leeds. We offer both prime and choice New York steak. If you'd like a companion to join you for dinner, I'd be glad to accompany you." She hikes her shoulder toward him suggestively.

"That's quite an offer." Everett doesn't crack a smile. Way to go, Judge Baxter. He knows how to ruin a person's day both on and off the bench. And right now, I'm not too sorry about it. "But I'm here for the auction. A friend of mine extended the invitation." He looks to me. "She said there would be cookies delivered fresh by the best baker in town."

Naomi takes him by the arm. "Right this way." And they're off before I can say a word in response.

Keelie rattles my arm as if she were trying to revive me. Trust me, it's not necessary. "Did you see that? He was flirting with you! That's the guy from the Honey Pot the other night."

"That's the judge who sided with me in small claims court. Mr. Sexy."

Keelie makes a squeaking sound while digging her nails into my forearm. "He is so into you! It looks like he wants to side with you in far more interesting places than a courtroom—like your bedroom."

"I don't have a bedroom." I raise my brows at my lust-filled friend. "Not technically, anyway. I'm in Lainey's guest room with all her dusty stuffed animals she couldn't stand to part with. Poor Pancake thinks he's in a taxidermy shop. The oversized giraffe with the large glass eyes has been giving us both nightmares for a week." I shudder just thinking about it.

"I'm betting Mr. Sexy could find a way or twelve to soothe and calm you."

"Who needs soothing and calming?" a male voice

strums from behind, and we turn to find Noah Fox looking every bit the wily animal his surname suggests.

Keelie's jaw unhinges at the sight of his fitted Italian suit, those glossy dark shoes, that glossy dark hair.

"Holy hello." Keelie takes a firm step back to properly take him in. "Detective Noah Fox, you are a sight to behold. Feel free to do a firm and thorough pat-down of either of us this evening. You never know where we might be hiding evidence you'd like to have your way with."

I kick her shoe, and she makes a face at me.

Keelie clears her throat. "I'd better check on the cookies." She takes off, and it's just Noah and me. It feels half as awkward and off-putting as it did in the beginning and yet still very awkward and off-putting.

"Cookies?" His face smooths out, and as soon as his lime green eyes hook to mine, my heart thumps into my throat without my permission. Probably just nerves. Mora Anne will undoubtedly be here, and I'm not too sure how she'll feel about seeing me. "You bake them?" There's a gleam in his eyes as if he were ready to come up with some acrid quip.

"Yup. Four dozen maple leaf sugar cookies, three dozen snickerdoodles, three dozen butterscotch chip cookies. Those last two were a personal request from the deceased's sister. She let the event coordinator know she would like to have them here."

"Well, I happen to love snickerdoodles"—he holds an arm out, and my mouth falls open as I thread mine through it—"and I happen to love maple leaf sugar cookies, and I have a soft spot for butterscotch. It happens to be my favorite."

"Duly noted," I say as we enter the grand ballroom in all its autumn glory. The hall is packed with people, so many that I'm not sure where they all came from. Honey Hollow doesn't have this many residents on a good year. In the corner to our right I spot Mora Anne and a stocky man speaking in a frenetic manner. "Ooh, look at that." I give Noah's arm a tug, and he leans in until he spots them.

"Mora Anne," he says it warm against my hair, and a shiver runs through me.

"I can see why you're so sought after, detective. Your investigative skills are to be admired." I can't help but tease him. It feels as if Merilee's killer should have been arrested by now, and yet we've hardly gotten out the gate.

"And that red-faced and angry man next to her is Moose Hagan." A smug grin rides over his face. "Any relation to your ex-boyfriend Bear?" He lifts a brow.

A choking sound emits from me. "What? No. Not that I know of. And have you been investigating me?"

"Nope," he flatlines. "I stopped in for dinner last night at the Honey Pot. Keelie filled me in on all the juicy details before I had a chance to order my meal."

That doesn't surprise me. I do a quick scan of the room, ready to chop off my best friend's head for turning over all the dirty details. A breath gets caught in my throat as I look back to him with a newfound fear. "She didn't happen to mention—"

"New York?" he cuts me off with an amused gleam in

his eyes. "No." His affect falls once again, and I'm glad about it. A gloating Noah Fox is more than I can handle.

"So, who's Moose Hagan?" I redirect his attention back to the party and far away from any out-of-state dalliances I might have had. "And did Keelie offer him up on a silver platter, too?"

He tips back on his heels as we inspect the two of them still going at it. "Hagan works as a football coach in Leeds. High school ball. His name came up when I googled Merilee. They were at some of the same meetings together."

"You memorized every name at the district educational meetings?" Merilee was a part-time substitute. I suppose it helped with the bills. The business really was struggling.

Naomi walks by and does a double take in our direction before stopping. "Hello, honey." Her shoulders do a little swivel, and I roll my eyes. The way Naomi is tossing it out there tonight you'd think she were having a fire sale on her lady bits and pieces. Trust me, there is no sale. They are always set at a discount rate. "I didn't get your name." She smooths her hair before extending her hand, a plastic smile cropping up on her lips.

"He didn't give it." I twirl Noah to my right and put us in a more prime position to witness the meltdown Mora Anne seems to be having with Moose. "This isn't your run-of-the-mill grief. This is a full-on confrontation," I whisper.

"Noah Fox." Noah, the traitor, turns to shake Naomi's

long, skinny paw. "You wouldn't happen to know what that's about, would you?"

Naomi bats her lashes bashfully as if he just asked her to dance. "You mean Mora Anne and that football coach? I don't know, but I've seen him around the Manor a time or two."

"Here in Honey Hollow?" I lean in. "But he works all the way in Leeds. What was he doing here?"

"I don't know." Her face twitches with disdain for me. "I don't keep track of why people visit. They just do." Her fingers walk their way up Noah's arm as she giggles into him.

Wow. Naomi couldn't care less that we're practically connected at the hip. If I wasn't sure about Naomi's stance on me before, this says everything.

"Is that Merilee's boyfriend?" Noah sounds hopeful, and suddenly I'm very sorry for him and his prospective career as a private investigator. Everyone in Honey Hollow knows that neither of the Simonson sisters was dating. They were both too hostile and agitated to hold down a man, let alone find one that would tolerate them for a prolonged interval of time.

"Moose?" Naomi tosses that river of ebony hair over her shoulder. "Heck no, that would be Travis Darren." She averts her eyes. "My mother always said you can't trust a man with two first names."

True. Becca has said that a fair number of times that it probably should have sent up a red flag or two seeing that

Honey Hollow is low on such double-monikered creatures, but I digress.

"Merilee had a boyfriend? Are you out of your mind?" The words come out a little too fast, a little too loud, and a handful of people turn my way. "You take that back, Naomi. You can't lie about dead people and get away with it."

"I'm not lying. Merilee was seeing Travis for over a month now. His sister, Janet, told me. She wasn't too pleased. She said Merilee treated her like garbage."

"Well, that's par for the course." I try to steady myself on my feet. I still can't wrap my head around the fact Merilee was in a relationship, albeit short-lived.

Naomi's name chimes from the back, and she takes off glowering in that direction.

"A boyfriend?" I choke Noah's arm and take in a lungful of his sweetly spiced cologne in the process. "Can you believe it? I can't."

"No." He looks back to where Mora Anne now stands speaking to a small crowd of women. "I can't either."

A thought occurs to me. "Hey, how did you know so much about Moose? I mean, outside of the school meetings, what made him so remarkable?"

His cheeks flex as he turns his attention back to me. "Because Moose Hagan was Merilee Simonson's boyfriend."

"What?" I bounce on my heels. "There's no way either of you is correct. Obviously, the cider is spiked tonight."

"I didn't have a drop. The reason I was able to single

Moose out was because I sifted through a few public pictures of their events and found a small handful with Merilee and Coach Hagan looking a touch too cozy. So I drove down to Leeds and spoke with a few people. Finally had an assistant of his open up and mention the fact Coach Hagan announced two weeks ago he was leaving his wife of thirteen years, two kids in the mix."

"*What*? You think he was leaving her for Merilee? Merilee was a lot of things, but I can't see her as a home-wrecker."

Noah leans in with his left brow hooking into his forehead. "He mentioned her by name. Said he was ashamed how it all went down."

I suck in a quick breath and disconnect my hold on him in the process. "That sounds ominous."

"I thought so, too."

A jumble of bodies squeeze their way past us, and my purse feels as if it's about to hit the ground. No sooner do I secure it over my shoulder than I spot a neatly folded piece of paper tucked hastily near the opened zipper, glaring at me with its bright yellow hue. I pull it out and open it between us.

"I know what you did. Back off or else," I read and a chill prickles my skin as the words ring out. The letters are drawn out with sharp peaks and valleys, a distinctive look, but not one I recognize. "Noah, someone just stuffed this into my purse." I look frantically into the crowd, but there are so many limbs, so many glammed up bodies I hardly

recognize a soul. "Do you think the killer just delivered a message?"

Noah pulls a small plastic bag from his pocket and both quickly and discreetly takes the note from me and makes it disappear behind his lapel. "I think this is a clear sign you need to keep from asking questions around town."

"There's no way I'm doing that. I'm not going to let some lunatic intimidate me. Give me that note back."

Noah shakes his head, the defiance in his eyes assuring me he's not giving in without a fight. "Detective Lemon, you are officially dismissed from the case."

I'm so stunned I can't believe my ears. "What are you saying?"

"I'm saying stay out of my investigation."

CHAPTER 11

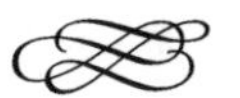

Noah Fox takes off into the crowd inside of the grand ballroom of the Evergreen Manor, and suddenly I really am moved to murder someone.

"How dare he!" I turn on my heels and smack into a body. Judging by the solid granite wall I don't need to look up to confirm my suspicions, but I do. "Are you always going to get in my way like that?" I take a full step back before Everett tries to walk through me once again.

"No." Everett smacks his lips as if he were bored with

me before craning his neck into the crowd. "How dare he what? What did Noah Fox do now?"

I open my mouth to say something but think better of it. No matter how much the truth is wanting to spill out of me like a greasy glass of marbles, I'm betting Everett will suggest I take Noah's advice. If it's one thing I can't stand, it's male camaraderie—especially when it maligns my intentions. For the record, my intentions are good. I just want to put Merilee's killer behind bars and be done with it. And now I have that note to contend with. Correction —*had* that note to contend with.

"Noah Fox just stole a piece of my private property before sauntering off into the crowd like he owned it." I spot Noah at the buffet line stuffing his face with my butterscotch cookies, amassing quite the confection collection on that little white plate he's holding.

Everett pushes out a quiet laugh. "That's Noah in a nutshell."

Just as I'm about to grill him into tomorrow with all the hellfire of a prosecuting attorney, Keelie steps in.

"Is this a private party? Or can anyone deliberate in your honorable presence?" Her teeth glitter as she bubbles with laughter. Keelie is adorable, and for whatever reason, every adorable ounce of her is annoying the heck out of me.

Neither Everett nor I bother to answer. Instead, I continue my interrogation of the questionably honorable judge.

"Is Collette Jenner the one who invited you tonight?"

"That she did." He rocks back on his heels while scanning the room as if looking for her.

"I thought you said she was your ex? It sure doesn't sound that way to me." I shoot Keelie the side-eye. We've never been good at maintaining a relationship with our exes, seeing that the original relationship didn't work out to begin with.

Everett grunts as if my line of questioning offends him on some level. "I'm on good terms with all of my exes. Collette invited several employees from the courthouse. The PR firm she works for is here in number, too." He openly glowers into a crowd of suits.

"Do I sense a smidge of jealousy?" I relish the thought. Even though I've only known him for a short time, I'm reveling in the fact something has gotten under his skin. Everett has been one hundred percent stoic and impossible to read since the beginning. I suppose that's why his profession suits him so well.

"Not a smidge, not a drop." He gives a dark chuckle as Noah steps into our small circle.

"What are you laughing at?" He takes an angry bite out of a bright orange maple leaf-shaped cookie. Fall is tied with spring as my favorite time of year. One of my favorite things to do this time of year is make a leaf cookie bouquet and pass them out to friends. I even gave one to Mora Anne and Merilee last year. Not because we were friends. Mostly I felt sorry for them, two spinster-like women holed up in that apartment of theirs all the time, but apparently Merilee was having a merry time with a married man no less.

Everett maintains his amused demeanor, which only seems to infuriate Noah. "I'm laughing at the fact you've already managed to tick Lemon off. Are you going for a record? Because I think you just broke one."

Noah ceases chewing his cookie, still shooting that death glare his way. The tension rises, as does the volume of the music once again, and I'm quick to jump between them in the event things decide to escalate quickly.

"Before you do something rash like slug him—Everett here happens to be a judge."

Noah gives one of those slow blinks that lets you know he's beyond exasperated. "I know all about him."

Keelie gasps, "How in the world? Let me guess. You landed yourself in a heap of fun-loving trouble and wound up in the honorable judge's courtroom?" The entire left side of her body takes the opportunity to lean against Everett's rock-hard body, and I can't help but frown.

We look to Noah awaiting a reasonable and perhaps slightly above the law response.

"First"—he stabs Everett with his glare—sorry analogy on my part, but accurate nonetheless—"why are you always around?"

Everett scowls ten times harder than before. "I'm an invited guest. I've bid on half a dozen items. Be glad I'm around."

"Around Lottie?" Noah doesn't relent in that heated stare.

Keelie ribs me, and I can't help but press my lips tight. I can't recall a single time when I've had this much testosterone-based attention paid to me. Not in Honey Hollow. For sure not in New York.

Everett pushes his tongue into his cheek, and you can practically see the steam rising from his ears. "What's it to you?" He takes a step in.

"Hey?" I push my hands between them. They're so close I can't help but land my palm over each of their chests. I can feel their heartbeats vibrating right up through my arm, and it tickles just enough. More importantly, I'm able to securely say that Noah Fox's chest is just as rock-hard as Everett's. Hey! Maybe they go to the same gym?

Everett leans in close, his attention still one hundred percent on the obnoxious PI. "Look, I'm not seeing Lottie, and I'm not out to steal her from under you."

Noah's cheek flickers as if he were embarrassed on some level.

"I'm not seeing anyone," Everett continues. "And I certainly don't want to see you. Why don't you leave? You and I both know you're not parting with one red cent to help that poor woman bury her sister."

Noah flinches. "I'll have you know I just bid two hundred dollars for the sundry basket. It comes with toothpaste, and mouthwash, and a boatload of toilet paper. You never know when you're about to step in a pile of bullshit. Or in my case, run into one."

Keelie and I gasp in unison.

"And on that note"—I spot Chrissy Nash standing next

to the oversized picture of Merilee, and she looks as if she's about to be ill—"I'm leaving. Until you two can grow up and, for the love of all things good, tell me how you know each other—the two of you can have at it." I pull Keelie along with me, not giving her a say in the matter.

"Hey!" she's quick to protest. "It was just getting to the good part."

"I need you to help me solve this case. Noah wants me to stay out of the investigation, but it will be over my dead body." I grimace as soon as I say it. For sure I'm not telling Keelie about the note. The note may as well not exist as far as I'm concerned. I need to solve this mystery or in the least put the white-hot spotlight on some other unfortunate soul. I'm their only suspect for goodness sake.

"Chrissy!" I muster all the enthusiasm I can before realizing something far more somber would have drawn less suspicion. "How are you? I haven't seen you in ages." I offer an impromptu embrace.

"I'm fine." She casts a glance to Merilee's picture. "I just wish Merilee was fine, too." She pushes a tissue to her nose as her eyes well with tears. There are bags under her eyes, and her face is blotchy as if she's been weeping for hours.

"You don't look so fine. And understandably so. It's terrible what's happened."

She nods while swallowing down her grief. "I just wish we had left off on better terms." She waves it off. "It was a stupid little squabble about a parking space."

"Is that what you were arguing about that day at the orchard?" The visual comes back to me—Chrissy Nash,

Eve Hollister, and a third woman I couldn't identify. They all looked a bit frazzled that day. Mora Anne included. "And who was that woman standing with you? Was that Laurie Ackerman from the library? She works with my sister." I know for a fact it wasn't Laurie because she's due to have a baby any day now and is on bed rest. Lainey mentioned last week she couldn't find a replacement for her.

Chrissy opens her mouth as if to speak, then promptly closes it. "Um, yes, I guess that was Laurie." She shakes her head as if her own body were protesting the words that just flew from her mouth. "Like I said, it was just a silly argument over a parking space." She speeds through the hall and into the lobby.

Keelie blows out a breath. "Well then. That wasn't suspicious at all." She ticks her head to the exit. "I think we have a suspect, Detective Lemon."

I spot Everett and Noah speeding this way.

"And we're not going to say a word to anyone else." I manufacture a smile just as they close in on us.

Noah takes a deep breath, and his chest expands for a mile. "We're ready to tell you how we know each other." He pushes each word out as if he were moving a boulder, and my curiosity is piqued twice as much as it was before.

Everett's shoulders sag as if he too were acquiescing. His serious eyes settle over mine as if he were about to deliver devastating news. "We're brothers."

A hand pulls me from between the two of them and

whisks me into the thick of the crowd, past the tangle of endless bodies, and right into the center of the dance floor.

A pair of arms wraps themselves around me, and I look up at that familiar devious grin as we begin to sway.

"Otis Fisher!" I playfully tap his foot with mine. "You have always had the worst timing."

His lids turn to slits as he breaks out into a lazy grin. "It's the first slow song of the night, and you promised me a dance."

I'm about to correct him but then remember his kind offer to help me with the office furniture. "I guess one dance couldn't hurt."

"That's better." He touches his chin to the side of my head. "And it's *Bear* to you."

"You got it, Bear." It comes from me lackluster as I look to the spot where I was standing just a few moments ago with Everett, Noah, and Keelie, and now all three of them have dispersed. I do a quick scan and spot Keelie speaking with Lainey, the two of them glancing my way with disapproval.

But Everett and Noah are nowhere to be seen.

They're gone.

Brothers.

I can't seem to comprehend it. That solves the surface mystery, but there is a fissure between them that runs much deeper—something damaging that has absolved any outward sentiment of brotherly affection.

Everett is stubborn. Cold as iron.

Noah is most definitely stubborn. Ornery as hell.

I'm going to get to the bottom of the rift that's torn them apart.

Just like I'm going to get to the bottom of whoever slipped that note into my purse so brazenly. I'm betting they're the same person who killed Merilee Simonson.

I'm not staying out of Noah Fox's investigation because, for one, it never belonged to him. I found the body. I'm the number one suspect. It's up to me to clear my name.

I'm kick-starting my investigation bright and early tomorrow morning, and I'm starting with Eve Hollister. If Chrissy won't tell me the truth about that mystery woman, maybe Eve will.

After all, why would Eve lie to me?

Why would Chrissy?

CHAPTER 12

The Honey Pot is filled to the brim with my mother and her cohorts as their cheeky book club commences for the day. The air in the Honey Pot is thick with the scent of fresh morning coffee, and the sweet scent of syrup permeates the room as patrons fill the seats in hopes to fill themselves with one of our scrumptious breakfast selections.

The book club peeps are a riotous bunch with their explosive bouts of laughter and their just as sudden pensive lulls. This month's literary selection has a woman in a billowy dress on the cover while a villainous looking man with a sharp goatee chases her through a valley. *The Viscount's Wench* was my mother's saucy pick. I know so because she furnished both Lainey and me with fresh copies from the bookstore right after she chose her spicy selection. My copy is sitting at the bottom of a box in Lainey's garage without much hope of retrieval. I can hardly think of unpacking, let alone reading. For sure I can't wrap my head around moving. All I can think about these days is who killed Merilee Simonson. You might say it's consuming me. And it's probably a good thing too since I was most likely threatened by the killer myself last night.

That note comes back to me, bright yellow, tucked aggressively into my purse, my personal property. That clear invasion of my personal space let me know they're not afraid to get in my face, without actually revealing theirs. Before I left, I asked Naomi if the Evergreen Manor had security cameras in the ballroom and was met with an enthusiastic no. Shutting me down in any capacity has always been Naomi's favorite thing to do, so the enthusiasm in general didn't surprise me.

"More coffee!" my mother sings as she flags me down. Since my mother's club is close to thirty strong, and they seem to require more attention than your average customers, I usually make it a practice to tend to them myself, freeing up the waitresses to focus on the tourists and regulars alike.

I do a quick round of refills as the women chatter

among themselves. Most have already leashed their purses to their shoulders signifying an upcoming mass exodus. Eve Hollister and Chrissy Nash hold what appears to be a casual conversation with a couple of women on the end. I'm secretly hoping Chrissy will leave so that I can corner Eve before she takes off, too. I have to get to the bottom of this and find out who that mystery woman was that day at the orchards. I couldn't believe my ears when Chrissy entered into a blatant lie about Laurie Ackerman. I had Lainey call to confirm the fact she was still in fact bedbound.

"Lottie!" Mom claps her hands together dramatically, and I can feel the onset of a ripe embarrassment coming as sure as a thunderstorm. "Your pumpkin spice coffee cake was to *die* for! Do tell us your secret." She gives a playful wink. My mother's mission in life is to praise and uplift her daughters, but as it stands, that often goes hand in hand with a mingling of public humiliation.

My cheek flinches as she lets the morbid analogy fly, and at least a handful of women offer sideways glances in my direction. It's no secret that I'm the one that found Merilee. It's also no secret that I was taken to court by the sisters and brutally evicted the morning before her body was discovered. I'm not too sure anyone in Honey Hollow thinks I'm capable of murder, but considering the fact that it was most likely someone from our sweet town who plunged the knife into Merilee, I'm as good a suspect as any.

"Thank you, Mother." I offer the ladies around her a

crimped smile. “My secret is there’s love in the mix. I can’t imagine a day without baking. It just makes me happy.”

An echo of coos circles around the table as the women surrounding my mother look up at me as if I just gave birth to a puppy in front of them. The funny thing is, I’ve never quite envisioned myself having a human child. Growing up, while my friends and sisters were playing mommy with baby dolls, I was the pretend mother to an entire litter of puppies and kittens. I always thought I’d end up with a dog one day, but when Nell said she needed to place one of the kittens she picked up, I took one look and knew he was the one for me. Pancake and I have been family ever since.

One by one the women gather their belongings, and as fate would have it, Mayor Nash comes in for his morning cup of coffee and usual cowboy omelet. It doesn’t take long for Chrissy to notice her ex and bid a spirited adieu to her book-loving besties before dashing out into the brisk morning air. Eve says goodbye to a couple of women before leaning over to pick up her tote bag brimming with copies of *The Viscount’s Wench.* Most of the ladies have made it a habit to donate their paperbacks once they’re through. And I see this as my golden moment.

“Are those books for the library?” I force my affect to brighten. Eve has always known me as a cheery person, and this isn’t the time to show my newfound suspicious side. “I’m heading that way in a bit to have lunch with my sister.” Sort of true. Although my cheeks heat as if brushed with brimstone. I have never been a good liar. There’s a reason I’m not starring in Hollywood movies.

Eve bucks a moment as her fingers spread wide. Eve Hollister has always been an animated woman. She's exactly my mother's age but looks as if she has ten years on her easily. Her hair is a shock of white, the bags under her eyes have evolved to full-blown suitcases the size of water balloons, and she's made a habit of wearing too much foundation to cover up the fact, but it only seems to make the lines on her face more prominent. Time and fate have not been kind to Eve. She lost her husband early in their marriage and spent the rest of her time focusing on her children. I think that commonality bonded her and Mother more than anything else. Then last year she had a health scare that had her name at the top of every prayer chain in the state, but she powered through that just fine.

"Why yes, you may. That's so kind of you." She hands me the overladen tote brimming with remnants of a forest. "Have you read the book? Please feel free to take a copy for yourself and even a few for your friends." She leans in and a silver lock of hair swings between her eyes like a sickle.

"Oh, I have a copy and so does my sister, but I'll ask around in the back before I get the surplus to the donation center." I bite down hard on my lip as she hastily puts on her chenille cardigan, a deep forest green. "Say, can I ask you a question?"

"Anything." Her head ticks back an inch, and there's a sparkle in her blue eyes as if the attention were feeding some underlying emotional need and I have no doubt it is. Eve's children all moved to Ashford years ago, and all she's had to keep her company are the characters in the novels she reads. According to my sister, Eve is a voracious reader.

I give a quick glance over her shoulder at my mother who seems to be engrossed in a conversation of her own. "Remember that day at the orchard—the day Merilee was killed?" I wince even bringing it up, as does she. As much as I want to come right out and ask her who that woman was standing with her that day, I don't think it's the best approach. "Someone said there was a woman asking the secretary about a cookie bouquet, and I think it may have been that woman you and Chrissy were with. Would you happen to know her name? I'd hate to have a customer upset with me because of a delayed delivery."

"What woman?" Her fingers claw at the gold chain around her neck.

"You and Chrissy Nash were speaking to the Simonson sisters just as I arrived. It looked pretty heated." Stupid, stupid me. Why would I bring that up? I'm sure Eve is working hard to forget the dirty details of that day just like everyone else. "Anyway, she was standing there with you. I thought it might be her."

Eve straightens, stiff as a corpse. Her baby blue eyes glaze over as if she's just seen her dead husband pop up behind me.

"Oh goodness, I can't remember a thing about that." She flings a black and white checkered scarf around her neck and weaves through the furniture. "I've got a doctor's appointment in less than ten minutes. If you'll excuse me, I need to make tracks." She speeds out of the

Honey Pot so fast you'd think I just threatened to set her hair on fire.

Mom comes up as the rest of the ladies clear out. "What was that about?"

"I think maybe Chrissy Nash and Eve Hollister are covering up a murder."

Mom tips her head back and chortles as her blonde curls spring over her shoulders. She's donned a bright orange pea coat and looks as fashionable as ever. My mother does love to dress for the seasons, and she looks every bit the autumn queen.

"Please, Lottie. Those women would no more house a murderer than you or I." She makes a face. "And don't worry, Lottie. I don't believe for a minute you're capable of doing something so heinous. Although, I might be the only one at the moment."

"Mother." I shudder at the thought of being the town lunatic. "That's exactly why I need you to do me a favor, to clear my good name."

"Anything." She leans in and takes up my hand. "You know I'd move the moon for you."

"Good. Because judging by your stubborn friends, you just might have to." I fill her in on the odd conversation Eve and Chrissy were having with the Simonson sisters that day along with the mystery woman I couldn't quite identify. And then I fill her in on how evasive both Eve and Chrissy have been. I omit the white lie Chrissy shed in a moment of discomfort. Just the thought of a murderer running free in Honey Hollow has just about everyone on edge. I can forgive her for that.

Mom's shoulders square out, her head held high. "Don't you worry, Lottie. I'll have this wrapped up by this afternoon. Whoever this mystery person is, I'll have her name to you in no time."

"You really think they'll open up to you just like that?" I'm afraid my mother isn't quite aware of what her friends are capable of. It seems that no sooner did fall come around than the dark side was ushered out of everyone in this tiny part of the country.

She gives an affirming nod. "I have my ways, Lottie. I'll have one of them singing like a canary in a coal mine by dinner. Just you wait and see." She dots my cheek with a kiss before speeding out the door.

I hate to be the one to break it to her, but canaries in coal mines don't usually sing. They die. And a part of me is terrified I may have inadvertently put my mother in grave danger.

Hours go by slow as molasses in January, and just as I'm beginning to think my mother's talent of wrangling even the most delicate information from an unsuspecting person has subsided, my phone buzzes. It's a text from my mother with just two words.

Melissa Hagan.

CHAPTER 13

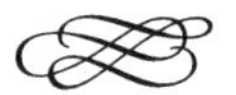

Melissa Hagan.

After an hour and a half of relentless breakneck baking, I leave the leaf-shaped cookies on the rack to cool while I—correction—while Keelie makes a quick phone call.

"Hello?" chimes the sweet voice of a female on the other end.

I nod to Keelie with the go ahead. She's in the know as

far as who the mystery woman is. In fact, she was the mastermind of this newly-hatched plan.

"Yes, hello! This is Keelie from the Honey Pot Diner out in Honey Hollow. We had a giveaway last night for a bouquet of cookies, and the winner said she couldn't take them. She, uh..." Keelie looks to me, baffled.

"Had a toothache," I whisper, shrugging simultaneously.

"She had a dental issue that prevented her from enjoying the scrumptious confections. Anyway, she said she was a friend of yours and asked that we deliver them to you instead. She said we could find you in the community directory. I have you on Myrtle Drive. Is that still a good address for you?"

Keelie listens intently, her penciled in brows dipping and rising with amusement. "Oh, I see. At your mother's." She motions for a pen, and I quickly pull out a grease pen and some parchment for her to write on. "1631 Grand Marque, Hollyhock. Well, that's just around the corner. I bet you've been down to Honey Hollow a time or two, haven't you?"

I shake my head frenetically at Keelie. There's no way I want to grill Mrs. Hagan over the phone.

Keelie hangs up and purses her lips at me. "She said she had to go pick up her daughter from school. I take it Honey Hollow isn't her favorite subject."

"Yeah, and we know why," I say as I begin to ice the cookies in haste. "Because she just corroborated the assistant coach's story. I guess Noah Fox really knows his stuff."

"I do know my stuff."

Keelie and I turn abruptly to find a sober-faced Noah Fox darken the entry to the kitchen, all decked out in a suit, which reminds me—he is supposedly Everett Baxter's brother. For some reason, that familial connection just doesn't seem to fit.

"Care to say it to my face?" He gives a brazen smile, and my blood begins to boil just seeing it.

"You took my note, and you told me to stay out of your investigation. I don't see a single reason for you to smile in my presence. And by the way, last I checked, the investigation belongs to the Ashford Sheriff's Department."

His chest pumps with a slow breath. "I happened to walk in just as you mentioned Mrs. Hagan corroborated the assistant coach's story. Therefore, it's safe to say you're not staying out of anyone's investigation."

"What note?" Keelie looks to me confused, and my mouth opens, ready to spew a half-truth, a lie, anything at all, but nothing comes out.

Noah heads over. "Somebody threatened Lottie last night." His eyes settle over mine, and an unexplained calm settles over me. "I followed you home just to make sure you were safe."

"You followed me home?" It comes from me astonished. "And you were eavesdropping on a private conversation just now. You're out of line." My voice hikes with anger. "You are a certified stalker, Detective Fox."

"Eavesdropping and following people happen to be in

my job description." His own voice hikes a notch, as those serious eyes remain trained on mine. And then at the drop of a hat he softens. "But you're right. I was out of line, and I apologize. I care about you as a person. I don't want you to be the next victim that this maniac butchers."

"Aww." Keelie's shoulders sag on cue as she coos into him.

"Fine." I box up the cookies—two sunflower yellow, two pumpkin orange, and two verdant green—and tie them up with twine. For the bakery that's to come next door, we've ordered pale pink boxes, unbleached boxes with windows as well, and I'm dying to see them. "I'm headed to Hollyhock." I shoot Noah a look sharp enough to pin him to a wall. "I suppose since you'll follow me there, I might as well hitch a ride and save some gas."

He sheds a crooked grin, that devilish gleam in his eyes shining right through. "Now we're getting somewhere." He heads out the front door, and I take a moment to glare at my gloating bestie.

"Don't worry, Keelie. I won't do anything you would do," I tease.

Her brow hooks into her forehead. "Why don't you do the opposite of what you would normally do and give us something to talk about for once?"

"You wish," I say, taking off after him.

"*You* wish!" she calls after me. "The best part is, you can make your wishes come true!"

THE DRIVE to Hollyhock is thick with silence. I can't remember the last time I was in a car with someone else, let alone someone else who happens to harbor an extra body part or three in his pants.

"There it is," I say as we come upon a log cabin style home. "1631 Grand Marque," I say as my heart vibrates straight through to my bones. I go to open the door, and Noah lands a hand over mine.

"Let me do it. If she's the killer, she won't take too kindly when you start asking questions. Trust me, whoever did it is paranoid right about now. I don't think that was your traditional psychopath. That looked like a classic crime of passion."

The slight look of pleading in his eyes tenders me into relaxing back in my seat a moment.

"But I'm a woman and she's a woman. Trust me, she'll feel a lot more comfortable seeing me on the other side of the door than a man with the body of a wrestler."

His head tips back, and I can practically see his ego going off like an airbag. "Wrestler, huh? Pro or high school?"

"Definitely pro." I shake my head at his willingness to have his ego stroked. And seeing that he's a man, I'm betting he's eager to have something else stroked as well.

I suck in a quick breath as I pull my head straight from the gutter. It's not Noah's fault he's a stunning specimen of a man. But, unfortunately, he is squarely to blame when it comes to controlling that stubborn streak that seems to be embedded into his soul.

"Look"—I say, getting out of the truck—"if you stay in the car like a good doggy, I might just give you a treat." My fingers clasp over the door as I'm about to shut it. "I'll let you know what I've garnered in my investigation."

"Exchanging notes. I like that." His eyes light up, and I can't help but think he's mocking me somehow. I shut the door, not nearly as enthusiastically as I want to, and make my way up to the cute little cottage with its chimney chugging powder gray smoke into the air. A bed of auburn and butter yellow mums lines the walkway, a ghost white pumpkin sits on the porch giving it a warm inviting feel, and two twin wreaths comprised solely of acorns decorate the front doors.

I give the doorbell a quick buzz, and it takes less than ten seconds for a watery figure to emerge behind the frosted glass. The door swings open, and a petite brunette with her hair in a bun smiles wide.

"Oh my goodness! You must be from the Honey Pot. Come in and set those down. I was just planting some flowers out back, and I'm afraid I have soil all over me." She leads me through an impeccably beautiful interior with pale wood floors. A giant fake bear rug lies draped over a leather sofa in the living room, and there's a flannel moose head hanging over the fireplace. She leads us into an expansive kitchen filled with enviable stainless steel appliances, commercial grade, and a kitchen island made of powder white marble. "I bet it was my good friend Chrissy who sent them. She's been nothing but a rock for me."

Chrissy Nash!

"Oh? Did something happen?" I try to sound shocked and concerned as if I'm just hearing about a disturbance in her life. Not that I know her enough to warrant such a reaction, but we're all human. In that sense, it's totally compassionate of me to be concerned. "I mean, your family is okay, right?" Too close to home? I can't help it. She walked into that one.

"It's nothing like that." She rinses her hands under the sink before patting them dry on a towel. "Actually, I guess it very much is something like that. My husband thought it was a good idea to run out and find himself a girlfriend." She rolls her eyes as if it were one of those annoying things that husbands eventually get around to doing. "Other women might have been more tolerant, but I'm not that kind." She takes the cookies from me and pulls off the twine with minimal effort. I'm always careful not to wrap anything too tight. I figure if you purchase something as delicious as this you want to tear into it and not have to fight your way through aggressive packaging. "Would you look at that?" Her entire face brightens. "These are adorable. I think I'll save them for the kids. Let me give you something for the trouble."

"Oh no, please don't."

She gives a quiet laugh as she pulls her purse from off the counter and quickly rummages through it. "Looks like I don't have any cash on me." She pulls out a couple of orange rectangular coupons. "How about tickets to a football game out in Ashford? I seem to have a plethora of those." She glares at the tickets as if they were her cheating husband before passing them to me. "It's high school ball, but some people get a kick out of that. No pun intended. They're for tonight."

"Perfect." I run my fingers over them as if they were made of gold. "I mean, I think I'll really enjoy seeing the game, and I know just the friend I'll bring with me."

"I'm glad to hear it," she says, walking me to the door.

I step back out into the autumn chill and tug at my flannel as the frigid air licks my skin.

I take another look at the poor woman whose husband left her for Merilee Simonson, or at least attempted to.

"I'm really sorry about your husband. Maybe there is no girlfriend?" I shrug because I happen to know that technically there isn't a living one, at least not Merilee. "I mean, maybe there's a shred of hope of putting your family back together. You never know, right?"

Her entire frame stiffens as she shoots a cold glance into the forest across the street. "There isn't a girlfriend anymore, that's for sure. And I for one am darn glad about it, too." Her lips pull back into a malevolent smile, and my blood runs cold at the sight.

"Did you know her?" My heart thumps erratically. My hands begin to shake. "The girlfriend?"

She looks past me once again, her stare strangely vacant

as she continues to glare across the street. "I met her once. That was all I needed."

"All you needed."

The door slams shut between us with a violent bang, and I stand there stunned a moment before getting back to the truck.

"I hope you don't have any plans tonight," I say, breathless, as I put on my seat belt. "I'm taking you to a football game."

He twitches his lips as if considering a smile. "Sounds like a date."

"It's not," I assure him.

"Fine. I hope you don't have any plans this afternoon. I'm taking you to grab a quick bite."

"Sounds like a date." I shake my head wistfully.

"It's not." He gives a lazy wink as he pulls out onto the road. "I just happen to be hungry."

NOAH and I pick up a couple of sandwiches at the Hollyhock Deli before heading to the park that overlooks a golden meadow. The wheatgrass below lights up like a fire as the sun begins to dip behind the thick pines on the mountain in the distance. A single lone oak with its leaves red as a blaze sits all by its lonesome in the vast expanse like a burning bush.

"So tell me about your brother." I can't help but bite

down over my lip as we sit on a bench with a premier view of autumn's splendor.

"Everett." He closes his eyes a moment and takes a breath. "He's not my brother. Not really. He's my stepbrother. Used to be anyway." He takes a bite out of his sub, and I can't help but note the way his jaw clenches and grinds in an angular manner that only seems to add to his comeliness. One thing is for sure. I've never met a man quite like Noah Fox—or his stepbrother for that matter.

"So, what does that mean? Your parents were together for a time and then went their separate ways?"

"Divorced." He winces. "My father married his mother back when we were in high school. My younger brother, Alex, and I moved out to Fallbrook. Let's just say Everett and his sister weren't so welcoming. They couldn't see the good in my father." He bows his head a moment as he examines the ground. "Can't say I've ever seen it either. Anyway, they were right. Dad pilfered Everett's poor mother for everything he could before ditching out of town. Left my brother and me to fend for ourselves after the divorce. My brother went into the Marines, and I went to school, worked full time to get through it. Had a few roommates too many, but I made ends meet and graduated on time. Did my graduate work at Ohio State."

"And that's where you met your ex?" I ask cautiously. I of all people understand how thin the ice is in that end of the pond.

"Exactly. So you see, I am not, and never will be, Everett Baxter's favorite brother."

"I'm sorry to hear that—all of it. I guess I can understand why Everett would be upset with your father, but I still don't think that's any reason to treat you that way." I take a bite out of my sandwich, but my gaze never leaves his. Noah's eyes are magnetic, twin green marbles that throw shadow and light, and it's as if my own eyes don't want to miss the show.

"That's very nice of you to say. But we had our differences, too. High school was a trying time in general, and I sort of walked up on his turf. He was one year ahead of me in school, but it still made for tight quarters. He's a judge now, though." He shakes his head as if he can't believe it. "He's made a success of his life, and I've made a mess of mine. I believe he predicted that way back when. I've always hated disappointing people." His chest rumbles with a dark laugh.

"That's a terrible thing to say." A moment bounces by with the two of us lost in one another's eyes.

"Tell me about New York. Not about Columbia. About what really happened." He gives a sober nod.

"Boy, you're really gifted when it comes to reading people, aren't you?" I set my food aside and scoot in closer as the breeze whistles around us, cold as the blade of a knife. I take a breath and look out across the meadow as the grass blows in waves, and I want nothing more than to dive in and forget all of my problems. "His name was Curtis. Graduate student. Business school." I pull my legs up on the bench and hug my knees. "I thought that was it.

After I left Honey Hollow and the heartbreak Bear imparted—"

"Bear? You mean Otis Fisher? The guy currently taking a sledgehammer to the loan department next door? He's been in my office a few times trying to repair the cracks he's made."

"That would be him." It takes all of my strength to admit it. Deep down, I'm still a little more than upset with Bear. "Bear cracked my heart way back when, and I thought it was the end of the world until Curtis shattered it to pieces. It made anything I went through with Bear feel like a day at the amusement park—all of the rides made me want to vomit, but still. Curtis proposed." My face grows so hot I'm sure my cheeks are about to combust. I'm pretty sure there is not a more hideous sight in the world than sitting next to someone whose head spontaneously bursts into flames. "Anyway, I called it off after my roommate decided Curtis might like her bed better. I came home early from work and found his wallet on the floor. His clothes were tossed around the floor like dirty laundry, and then I found something far dirtier on her mattress than I ever wanted to see." I glance to the amber sky reflectively. "My roommate just had her boobs done. Did you know they don't move the same afterwards?"

Noah barks out a laugh that quickly softens to something sorrowful. "I'm sorry. That was a terrible thing that happened to you. You're better off without him."

"I know, but as pitiful as it sounds, it took me a while to get that through my thick head. I guess I've always felt like a castoff, unwanted, unlovable. Deep in my heart I knew Curtis and I were too good to be true." Tears come uninvited, and I'm quick to blink them away. "My mother left me in a firehouse when I was just a few hours old. Not a stitch of clothing on. Still had my umbilical cord attached." I wipe a lone tear away before it has the chance to roll down my cheek. "My dad found me, took me home, and *the rest is Lemon family history* as my mother likes to say."

"And that's how you became Lottie Lemon." He examines me with a warm smile, his tender eyes taking in my features. "That's a beautiful story. And you're wrong. You are no castoff. It was a great mercy you ended up in that firehouse that day. The Lemons sound like wonderful people."

"They are."

The wind picks up with a violent force and blows our napkins all over the place as if they were confetti. Noah and I laugh while chasing down every last one. We put our food away and start in on a walk around the trailhead that leads to a viewpoint through the forest to our left. The winding dirt trail is rife with rocks and pinecones, so Noah takes up my hand as we head up. His fingers are warm and sure, strong and thick, and I drink down the feel of them against my own. We get to the top and his grip loosens a moment, but I firm my grasp over his.

"It's okay," I say it so soft the wind carries my voice right up into the boughs above us. "I don't mind."

The hint of a smile twitches on his lips as his hand tightens a bit over mine.

"Good. I don't mind either."

Noah and I walk to the edge of the scenic lookout, hand in hand, my heart doing its best to drill right through my chest, my adrenaline hitting its zenith. But we don't look out at the golden glory below us. We're not at all interested in this new vantage point to examine the majesty nature has on display. Our gaze remains firmly locked on one another.

Noah leans in, and my eyes widen a notch. It's happening. Noah Corbin Fox is going for the kill, and I can't help but hold my breath in anticipation. A smile twitches on his lips as he bows in and brushes his lips over mine with a barely there pass, and my body pulsates with a heartbeat all its own. A sudden wave of dizziness hits me as my eyes remain closed, and I would swear on all that is good and right that the world just swayed beneath my feet.

He pulls back as his Adam's apple rises and falls. "I would apologize, but I'm not in the least bit sorry."

My lips part, but nothing comes out as a laugh gets locked in my throat. "Me neither." I hike up on my tiptoes and press my lips to his and feel their softness before I open for him and let him in. Noah Fox kisses me tenderly, sweetly, and then with a greater intensity, something darker and deeper. There have been many kisses in my life, but none as beautiful, none this alive and electrifying.

Noah and I spend a couple of unapologetic hours with our arms wrapped around one another, our bodies sealed at the lips.

The ground spins beneath my feet again, and I wrap my

arms around him to keep from falling. But I'm falling in a far different way. I can feel it. No matter how much I swore it would never happen again, it's too late.

It's happening.

And I can't do a thing about it.

WE'RE LATE to the game, missing the entire first half. But we cheer with the crowd as the Ashford Spartans beat their crosstown rivals. I watched Coach Hagan as much as I did the game.

"This is great," I say as we head to the field long after the stands have all but cleared. "He'll be in a good mood. I bet we can ask him anything."

"That's the thing." Noah pulls his hand from mine and takes a few giant steps ahead while walking backwards. "You're going to stand safely on the sidelines while I do the talking. If he's the one we're after, there's no way I'm putting you in harm's way."

"Aren't you adorable." I can't help but frown as I speed past him. "But I don't need you to protect me, Noah. I can handle myself. I come from a long line of strong women." At least those that I know of.

I spot Coach Hagan just finishing up an interview and pull the hood of my wool coat halfway over my face. "Coach! Just a few questions." I jog up to him before glancing back to where Noah looks on disapprovingly. "I'm with the *Ashford Times*. Where did you pull that last-minute energy from? The chips were down, but you rallied in that last half and came back to life." Chips were down? Are there chips in football? I think not. And came back to life? Well, at least that's heading in the right direction—onto my next topic, death.

He babbles on in something akin to Latin to me, and I nod along as if I understand everything about that long-drive, punt, Hail Mary of a conversation.

"Sounds great." I take a small step in. "I would like to offer my condolences. I understand a colleague of yours was brutally murdered in Honey Hollow. Do you have anything you'd like to say about that? Perhaps a word of comfort to her family? Is there a good memory you had of the victim that you would like to be made public?" Made public? Nobody wants their dirty laundry aired anywhere near their fellow neighbor! Maybe I should have let Noah work his dark magic after all.

Coach Hagan takes in a sharp breath and holds it as his attention drifts toward the empty stands for a moment. "You think you know someone. You give up everything, and then you find out it was all a lie," he says the word under his breath, and it's all I can do to strain to hear it. His jaw clenches. "Tell her family I'm sorry it happened. It's a terrible, terrible thing." He starts to walk off, and I jump in his path.

"It sounds like you really knew her." I need something else. Something that confirms he was angry enough to kill her, but my brain can't seem to spit out the right words.

He shakes his head as he steps around me. "Turns out, I didn't know her at all."

I watch as he disappears out the gate along with the trickling of what's left of the crowd.

Noah steps in beside me. "Well, Detective Lemon? What's the verdict? Is the coach a killer?"

"I think he just might be."

CHAPTER 14

The secret to a successful piecrust is not to skimp on the butter or shortening, whichever the recipe calls for. The key to a delicious crust is to not overmix after adding the chilled water to the aforementioned ingredients and flour. It is a delicate dance of well-timed, well-orchestrated ingredients that if done right will produce an amazing flaky crust that is guaranteed to melt in your mouth.

Some people choose to go for a run, get a massage, or

even veg out and watch TV to help alleviate the stress in their lives, but for me baking has always been my solace. I've found that the ingredients need me to make a successful dessert a reality, and in a way I need them, too.

"You kissed him?" Lainey shouts with an undue level of excitement as she hops into her stilettos. My sister might work in a library, but she's been known to glam it up on more than one occasion. By every definition, Lainey is the hot librarian.

Keelie leans against the baking counter, eager to hear once again all about that magical lip-lock, and I shoo her right back off. Thankfully, we're in the rear of the Honey Pot's kitchen, a safe distance from the prying ears around us. "Sorry." She swipes a piece of a chopped apple from the mixing bowl, already drenched in thick, rich caramel sauce and moans as she bites into it. The entire restaurant is filled with the heavenly scent of warm caramel apple pie. "Of course, she kissed him. I didn't raise no fool. That man is a force of nature to be reckoned with. She was simply showing him who's boss." Her lips curl, and I can practically see her undressing Noah in her mind's eye.

"For the record, he kissed me first. And well, I didn't want to be rude, so I kissed him back."

The two of them sigh in unison.

"You're both being ridiculous. It was nothing. It was just a kiss between friends, I guess." It sure didn't feel like nothing. My body still trembles just thinking about those oven-hot kisses we shared yesterday.

I shake myself loose from the thought. "Look, the Apple

Festival is less than two days away, and I need to get these pies done and delivered by Tuesday. Holland called and said he wants the pies there early to help set up."

Keelie and Lainey watch mesmerized as my fingers work slowly to lace the lattice over each and every cutie pie, and there are hundreds of them lining every surface area in the Honey Pot. I've only got a couple of ovens to work with, and, at that, it will take hours to bake all of these pies.

"Someone's changing the subject." Lainey puts down her purse for the first time in an hour and washes her hands to help.

"The subject should never be on me to begin with. Merilee was just buried hours ago, and her killer is still prowling the mean streets of Honey Hollow."

Keelie scoffs at the analogy. "Please, there's not a person who lives here who's capable of carrying out an act like that. Have you considered that it might be a total stranger? Some crazed psychotic from the city coming in for a tour of the orchard? I spoke with my father. He said there was an uptick in foot traffic at the apple farm that day."

"Your father still hasn't crossed me off the suspect list." I shoot her a sour look without meaning to.

"It's a formality," she over-enunciates the word because she's already repeated it to me a half dozen times.

Lainey stands across from me and ties an apron on. "So, who do you think did it?"

"I don't know." My mind swirls with the possibilities. "For sure I didn't have a thing to do with it." That long-departed orange tabby flits through my mind, and I give a guilty glance to both my best friend and my sister but don't breathe a word. The last thing I need is for them to question my sanity. Lord knows I've done that enough on my own. "Mom got Eve Hollister to talk, and it turns out, it was Melissa Hagan, Coach Hagan's wife. She's pretty petite. I don't know if she'd have the strength to plunge that knife in and out so fast and make a break for it. But then she did look fit. Coach Hagan was seeing Merilee. He all but confirmed it."

"So strange." Lainey tries to steal an apple slice from a cutie pie, and I bat her hand away. "I mean the fact you said Merilee potentially had two boyfriends."

Keelie grunts, "The fact she had one and I have none makes me question everything. She was so angry and bitter all the time. Is that what men are looking for? Angry and bitter?"

"Nope," a male voice rumbles from our left, and we look over to find a smiling Noah Fox. My heart thumps out a riot just for him as I smile back.

"Welcome to my kitchen, Detective. We were just going over suspects and motives. I'm thinking Melissa could have been angry enough to do it."

"I agree." He leans against the wall and folds his arms over that enormous chest of his. Noah is pretty fit, too. It's been mere hours since we last saw one another, and yet my mouth is already watering for more of those delicious kisses. "Anger can trump strength, I can assure you of that."

That note crops up in my mind, but I submerge it once again.

"Then there's Moose—Coach Hagan himself." I think on it for a moment. "He's determined to win on and off the field. He had that kind of a fire in his belly. Not to mention, his off-handed comment about people not being trustworthy still has me rattled." I told them all about it. Lainey thought I should have reported that to the sheriff's department right away, but I can't help but think something isn't clicking. "He's got kids, though. I can't see him throwing away his whole life just because he was scorned by a woman."

Keelie waves me off. "Prison cells are full of men just like that."

"She's right," Noah is quick to agree. "Then there's boyfriend number two."

Keelie shakes her head as she hurries to swallow down her next mouthful of caramelized apples. "Travis Darren? Naomi was wrong. I bet she mixed him up with Coach Hagan."

Lainey holds up a finger. "I bet you're right! Travis Darren could have been a code name for her real boy toy."

I groan at the visual. "And then there's—" I'm about to bring up one other name just as Noah interjects.

"Me." He blinks a sad smile my way. "I just got a call. Captain Turner wants me down in Ashford in a half hour to interrogate me."

"What?" the three of us cry out in unison.

"There's no way," I protest while struggling to remove

my apron. "I'm coming along. You had nothing at all to do with this."

"And that's exactly why I'm not worried about it. And you shouldn't be either. Stay here and bake pies. I'll be back soon enough."

"You can't stop me," I say, coming toward him, my fingers still fumbling to free me of the bird's nest I've just turned my apron strings into.

"And you can't change my mind." He bows slightly toward Keelie and Lainey before waving his way out the door. "I'll call you."

"You don't have my number!" I shout.

My phone bleats, and I head over to find a text.

I'm a detective, Lottie. I have my ways.

A laugh lives and dies in my chest. "He has his ways, indeed."

I get back to the all-important task of baking, and before long, Nell is standing in our midst.

"Well, girls?" Nell casts those beautiful sparkling blue eyes my way when she says it. "A little birdy just told me there was a delivery next door this afternoon."

"What?" I squeal so loud the head chef barrels over just to make sure an avalanche of apples wasn't crushing me. "I didn't even notice. How could this have happened right under my nose?"

Keelie gives a sly wink. "I made sure she didn't set foot outside the restaurant today."

Lainey offers a knowing smile. "And I made sure to be here for the big reveal."

"Shall we?" Nell holds out her arm, and I thread mine through it as we make our way next door where a shower of light pours into the night.

A breath hitches in my throat as I look past the construction workers finishing up for the day, past the debris of boxes and plastic wrapping lying over the floors, and I can't believe my eyes. In the back, I spot a bevy of gleaming stainless steel appliances as Nell leads us inside. The walls smell of fresh paint, glowing a butter yellow just the way I imagined. The refrigerated shelves are all more or less in place. And as we make our way to the kitchen, tears fall fast and furious as I take in the drop-dead gorgeous ovens, as I take in the size of the industrial mixer that is almost as tall as I am.

"It's too beautiful to comprehend. I can't believe you're going to give me the run of this place." I shake my head at Nell. "You won't regret it. I'll treat it as if it were my own. I'll love this bakery as much as I love—well, Pancake." We all laugh at that one, but it's true and we all know it.

"I'm glad to hear it." Nell pats her hand over mine. "But I'm afraid it will never open without one last thing, and it's up to you to provide it." She nods up at me solemnly. There's something she's saying with her eyes that I can't quite grasp, something important that supersedes words, and I can't quite put my finger on it. "It needs a name. And not just any name. A good one!"

Lainey and Keelie start shouting out all sorts of adorable monikers. Honey Hollow Bakery, Honey Sweet Treats, the Honey Jar Cookies and More, Honey Hollow

Sweet Shop, Desserts First, Desserts to Die For—and I quickly veto that last one.

"I don't know." I look around the place. "Those are all great names, except the one involving death." I shoot Keelie a look. "But none of them feel like this place."

Nell pulls me in close, her sweet face inching toward mine. "I don't want it to feel like this place. I want it to feel like your place. What means something to you, Lottie? I want this to be personal for you."

"Personal." I try to take it all in at once, and yet I can't get my head to believe any of this is real. "I don't know. This is all too wonderful for me. I don't know anything about naming a bakery, Nell. In fact, my mind is so warped from baking all those cutie pies I can't think straight. Everywhere I look I see a cutie pie. Cutie pie, cutie pie, cutie pie." I blow out a hard breath at the place, feeling both hopeless in finding a name and undeserving of such a great honor.

"Cutie pie." Nell feasts her eyes on every corner of this magnificent space. "I think it suits it, don't you?"

Keelie claps her hands. "The Cutie Pie Bakery!"

"The Cutie Pie Bakery." I try it out for size. "Oh my goodness, I think I love it."

The three of them break out in cheers.

"But wait, we'll be serving a lot more than pies. I mean, there will be cookies, and strudels, and brownies, and cupcakes, and macaroons, and bread puddings, and cobblers, and you name it. I plan on having it fully stocked. And *cake*! There will be lots of cake!"

Lainey lets out a breath as she cocks her head to the side. "How about a smaller sign that reads *fine confections, coffee, and more?*"

Keelie gasps, "That says it all!"

"The Cutie Pie Bakery," I say once again, this time with the hope that those words hold in them. "Fine confections, coffee, and more. I love it!"

The four of us jumble together in one long, tangled embrace, and I never want to let go.

It's perfect.

AN HOUR PASSES and Keelie gets to the business of bussing tables. Lainey went home to feed Pancake for me as I finished putting another batch of adorable little cutie pies into the oven. But there's not one ounce of me that wants to sit around waiting for those cute beauts to finish up. Instead, I head next door to their namesake again and make my way inside just as Bear and his cousin, Hunter, finish up for the day.

"It's coming together." Bear takes off his hat and shakes his dirty blonde curls loose. Emphasis on the *dirty*. Bear has always had the mind and mouth of a sailor. Not that I minded once upon a time, but times have changed.

"It sure is," I say under my breath, just trying to soak it all in once again.

Hunter slaps Bear over the shoulder. Hunter has always

been Bear's doppelgänger. If you didn't know better, you would think they were twins. The two of us have been on friendlier terms than Bear and me. "This guy right here is making it happen for you, Lottie. There were three jobs before yours and he sped you right through to the top."

My mouth falls open. "Otis Fisher! You keep surprising me."

He gives a quick wink. "And I don't plan on stopping."

The three of us head out into the cool night air and they take off for home, but I can't seem to tear myself away from this place. This is home, mine anyway.

The sound of furtive voices rising to the sky drift this way, and I spot two shadowed figures standing in front of the Busy Bee. One of them has on a long velvet skirt that catches the light of the streetlamp from down the way. I sneak across the street and tuck myself close to the buildings as I try my best to listen in. It looks as if Noah's eavesdropping disease is catching.

I lean out from behind the wall of the florist shop, and the figures come into focus. I squint over at the woman facing me and gasp.

It's Mora Anne!

A low and slow growl emits from the taller woman before she starts in again on Mora, and I recognize that Cruella de Vil knockoff as none other than her twisted cousin, Cascade.

"Don't you tell me what to do with my money," Cascade snips as she gets right in Mora Anne's face, and I'm half-afraid a fistfight might break out. "I don't need you, just like I didn't need your sister. I have all the authority I need to pull rank. You can't even keep this glorified box of ribbons opened. Why should I trust you to do something much bigger than you'll ever deserve?" She stalks off, and Mora Anne growls out a scream of frustration. My goodness, all of that on the day of her sister's funeral? As if she didn't have enough. Of course, the funeral itself was private. Gary at the funeral home was at the Honey Pot two days ago and said it would be small and that under no circumstances was I to crash it. As if. Although, admittedly I had thought about it. I did, after all, want to pay my respects.

Mora Anne starts stalking her way over, and I try my best to press into the woodwork behind me, but since that's not happening, I bounce right out into the sidewalk and bump into her.

"Oh, sorry!" I say, pretending I hadn't even seen her.

Spying and lying, both horrible traits I've taken on since my life has turned upside down. But I'm not the one who buried a sister today.

"I'm really sorry about Merilee," I say just above a whisper. "Heck, I'm sorry about everything. Is there anything I can do?"

Mora Anne scoffs, and for a second, I see Merilee there hiding in her face. That must be so painful to see the one you love in plain sight every day, and yet knowing you'll never speak to them again. Not in this world anyway.

"*Please*. You're not sorry. You're just like the rest of them. You hated my sister, and you hate me."

"Not true at all." I press my hand to my chest, pleading with her to understand. "I wish I could have been there to comfort you today. I'm very sorry you had to go through that. She doesn't belong there. She belongs here with us. I bet you miss her like crazy." I bite down hard on my lower lip to keep from spontaneously bawling. "What was that ruckus all about? I know that was your cousin, Cascade. I met her the day I left the apartment."

"Never you mind." She pulls on a pair of long black gloves in haste. "I'm sick and tired of you, and I'm sick and tired of my own family trying to steal what's mine." She stalks off down the street, alone and angry, and my heart breaks for her just a little bit more.

Merilee is dead, alone and in a grave. Mora Anne is dead on the inside, alone and in an isolative grave of her own making. She's so hostile and angry she can't even get along with her only living relation. But then, I have met Cascade. She's so mean she could slit your throat with just one look.

A breath gets locked in my chest.

And I wonder what else she's capable of doing with a knife?

CHAPTER 15

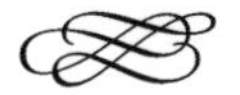

The Apple Festival is everything every single person in Honey Hollow needs it to be, filled with fun, food, family, and let's not forget dozens and dozens of caramel apple-filled cutie pies.

The sun is just getting ready to set and the sky is a heavier shade of blue, but the iced breeze doesn't let you forget which season you're in. The orchard itself is a grand backdrop to all the festivities. Buckets full of apples are scattered about, pumpkins dot every free surface, and the rich crimson leaves of the maples in the distance make this a feast for your eyes as well. It's wall-to-wall bodies here with hayrides to be had, games with stuffed animals to be won, cider to be pressed, and pumpkins to be launched out of a cannon. It's going to be a full week of revelry and fun for everyone of every age, and it truly looks as if every living soul in Vermont has turned out to help us celebrate.

Set in front of the barn, lined across checkered red and white linens sit hundreds of cutie pies for all to partake in. There's a line that goes around the barn and down near the parking lot just to get served up with one of those caramel delights.

"It was worth the wait," a male voice calls out from behind, and I turn to find Captain Turner in full uniform with a cutie pie nestled in his enormous hands. It looks as if it's the size of a quarter in that enormous mitt of his.

"Hey, Jack." I offer him a warm embrace, and he purrs with delight. I've never called him anything but Jack all my life, but seeing him in his official sheriff's duds has always made me want to call him Captain like everybody else.

"Talked to that boyfriend of yours the other day." His brow furrows with disapproval when he says *boyfriend.* This is usually the part where the logical part of me would protest that title, but not one part of me listens to that logical part. "I'm afraid I'm going to have to ask you to stop investigating the case. He says you've been openly questioning potential suspects. Lot, you know you can't go around doing that. You could be tainting the case. There's a very real chance the killer can go free because you're tipping them off that we're onto them."

My mouth falls open to protest, but he gently lifts a finger to stop me. "Now, now, don't go trying to defend yourself. I told you firmly in the beginning to stay out of it. I'm afraid if I find out you're meddling in my case again, I'll have to arrest you."

"Arrest me?" I'm dumbfounded by his brazen threat. But before I can lay into him—the man I have viewed as a father since my own passed away—he quickly dives into the crowd and is persona non grata soon enough.

I let out a roar of frustration.

"That's how I feel." A warm hand lands over my shoulder for a second, and I turn to find Everett looking every bit as somber as usual—and, well, vexingly sexy as his name suggests. He's donned his suit for the occasion and it makes him stick out like an Italian fitted sore thumb, but I'm sure the women here tonight will be thrilled nonetheless. His tie is charmingly red, and I'd like to believe he chose it just for the occasion. "I saw the line for your pies and wanted to let go of some steam just the way you did. But I figured I've got connections."

A weak smile graces my lips. "I suppose you do." I glare openly back at the crowd. "Where's Collette?" Collette Jenner has been a constant accessory whenever Everett is in town.

"She'll be here. She's working late tonight."

"Oh, that's right. She works for that fancy PR firm out in Ashford. I guess she's the big success she always threatened she'd be some day."

Everett's chest bounces at the thought as he gives a dull laugh.

"Judge Baxter! Is that the sound of laughter emitting from your throat? I don't believe I've had the pleasure to witness it before."

"That's what it is. But don't tell Collette. We may not be dating, but she's got a bite that stings regardless. I'm actually here tonight with Fiona."

"Fi-o-who?" I scan the crowd right along with him.

"Fiona Dagmeyer. I think you met her. She was the defense attorney walking out of the courtroom with me that day you were there."

"Oh yes, the stately brunette. Careful with that one. I can guarantee you she has a nasty bite. I'd make sure all your boy parts are intact once she's through with you. I saw her fangs all the way down the hall. I bet she sleeps upside down in her closet at night."

He barks out another laugh, much heartier and sincere than the last. "I'll keep an eye out for that. We're not together anymore, though. So I might just have to speculate alongside you about that whole sleeping upside down thing." He nods to me as his affect sobers up once again. "All right, Lemon. Let's have it. What had you howling at the moon just before I got here?"

I shoot him a vilifying look. "That stepbrother of yours."

"So, he finally filled you in on all the fun details, huh? What did he do this time? Steal your wallet and bolt out of town? Don't be too hard on him. It's hardwired in his genes."

"That's not funny. But in truth, it would have hurt less."

"What would have hurt less?" Noah himself appears before us, quick as an apparition, and if it weren't for the crowd he seemingly materialized from, I would have believed I was seeing dead people once again. I've only seen two, and those are both dearly departed souls I'd love to forget.

"You"—I jab my finger in his rock-hard chest—"plunging a knife into my chest." I freeze solid once the words leave my mouth. I can't believe I just said that not twenty feet from where Merilee met her fate the same way. "Why in the world did you rat me out to Captain Turner?" It didn't feel right calling him Jack at the moment since neither Everett nor Noah regards him as that. "He said he's going to have me arrested if I investigate this case. You know I have to clear my good name. And you know that I'm close to closing in on the real killer," I hiss that last part out in haste.

Noah's jaw clenches. "Correction—I am closing in on the real killer. You don't belong anywhere near this case," he says it calmly while crossing his arms across his flannel laden chest. No matter how much of a sucker I am for a man in jeans and a flannel—the red and black checkered variety, which happens to be my very favorite—I won't give in to his pompous ideals of where I belong. And judging by his

Neanderthal-like behavior, I'm guessing he'd say that was in the kitchen. "You belong safe in the kitchen"—he blinks an apathetic smile as if he were prying into my thoughts—"baking pies and all of those other tasty treats that give you so much pleasure to make for other people—not with lunatics that aren't afraid to wield a deadly weapon. I care about you, Lottie. And I don't want to see you getting hurt."

Everett takes a deep breath, and his suit expands right along with it. "I agree with him. I rather prefer you alive. People are unpredictable. Even the most unsuspecting soul can carry out a heinous crime. This investigation isn't for you, Lottie. Stay out of it."

"*AARRGGHHH*!" My entire body sizzles with anger. "I can't believe the two of you. Typical men trying to keep a woman down. Well, I won't let you. There's a killer out there, and I'm sick and tired of nobody doing a thing to catch them." I start to take off, and Noah grips me by the wrist.

"Lottie, wait," he pleads as he attempts to reel me in, but I free myself in haste.

"Don't you '*Lottie, wait'* me. I'm through with you, Noah Fox. I have never been a fan of being controlled by anybody, and the fact you went to Captain Turner to have me—*arrested* of all things—well, you just crossed a line, buddy!"

I take off and hear him shouting something about not trying to have me arrested. Potato, po-*tah*-to. He turned me in, same difference. I skirt the periphery of the festival just to get away from the thicket of bodies and come upon what I initially think is the best sight in the entire world, my best friend Keelie. But upon closer inspection, it's not Keelie. It's her emotional toad of a sister with her hair pulled back into a bun.

"Naomi," I say, stalking over. This day has already gone to hell in a handbasket, so I don't see what a minute with my favorite frenemy could possibly do to add to it. Besides, I have a burning question that I'm hoping she'll have the answer to. All night I thought about Merilee and her two beaus, and something just doesn't add up. "What do you know about Travis Darren? Do you think it could be a code name for Moose Hagan, a football coach down in Ashford?"

She flinches as if I struck her. "I've known Travis for years. He works as a leaf peeping guide in Hollyhock part of the year. Tall and lanky. I'm pretty sure he's no coach. He met up with a bear trap and about had his left foot snapped off. Walks with a bit of a limp."

Doesn't sound at all like Coach Hagan. That man practically ran the field with the boys on his team.

I shake my head at her. "Are you sure that it was Merilee who was seeing Travis Darren? I mean, don't you think that's a bit far-fetched? She already had one boyfriend." Whom I hope she dumped for the right reason, so that he could see what an idiot he was, tuck his tail between his legs, and go back to his wife and kids. Not that Melissa would take him back, but you never know, and it was the right thing to do. I'm proud of Merilee just because of it.

Naomi adjusts her red and white checkered dress while dancing in a pair of sky-high platform shoes. She's donned a pair of white statement piece earrings to go along with it, and as usual she looks as if she's trying too hard.

"Let me see." She shakes her head as she leans in hard. "Oh yeah, it *was* Merilee. I know this for a fact because I am *never* wrong." Her voice is loud and curt as her words blast over my face like a nuclear heat wave. That seems to be a raw talent of hers, going nuclear.

"Okay, geez. You were right. Per usual," I add as I make my way past her. No use in entertaining crazy. And besides, I have to admit the fact that both Mora Anne and Merilee look the same. Wait a minute. Maybe it wasn't Merilee meeting Travis Darren up at the Evergreen. Maybe it was Mora?

A dull laugh pumps from me with the epiphany. I bypass dozens of booths filled with oodles of people trying to check out the local flavor. Just about every business in Honey Hollow is represented here. Everyone but that fake one that belongs to that obnoxious fake investigator who probably got his PI license out of a vending machine that charged him a quarter.

The booth at the end has a banner above it that reads *The Busy Bee Craft Shop,* and I don't hesitate heading on over. The booth has a swarm of people in it ogling all of the knickknacks and potentially fun crafts projects poor Mora Anne hauled out on her own. But the table itself is left unmanned. Instead, a bright orange piece of paper sits neatly taped to the front. I step in close to read what it says, *Bee sure to stick around! I'll bee back in just a moment! -Mora Anne*

Wow, with all of those exclamation points and cutesy ways of spelling the word *bee*, you'd think you'd be treated to the warmest, bubbly soul on the planet upon her return. These people are in for a rude awakening.

I'm just about to step away when something about that note jars me.

"Wait a minute." My heart drums into my chest as I inspect the sharp peaks and valleys of Mora's neat penmanship.

"Oh my word." That threatening note I received tucked in my purse the night of the auction comes back to me. Whoever wrote that had the same jagged hand-writing.

I try to think back to any point in time where I could have been exposed to Mora Anne's handwriting, but can't think of a single instance. We weren't that friendly in school. There was no passing of the notes.

I glance outside the booth where the sky has suddenly taken on an eerie crimson hue, the color of blood, the color of certain death.

A flicker of a barely-there orange tabby cat garners my attention, and I gasp as I spot it twirling around the pole just outside of Mora Anne's booth. It pauses lazily before looking right at me. Those glowing yellow eyes look so hauntingly bright, it almost hurts to look right at them. It twitches its head toward the orchard and heads out in that direction.

So I do the only rational thing a person in my position would do.

I follow.

CHAPTER 16

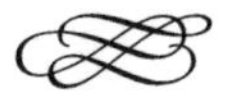

The riotous sounds from the crowd slowly fade away as a long, dead, rust-colored tabby leads me supernaturally to the right of the orchards where the sound of muffled voices comes from my right.

A man shouts something explosively loud, and the woman shouts back clear as crystal, "You'll live to regret it!"

An angry, tall, and lanky man limps his way out of the

orchard, and I hold my breath, waiting for the fallout, but he doesn't even seem to notice me.

That must be Travis Darren! Naomi nailed him to a T. How many other tall, lanky men with a limp could there be at the Apple Festival?

I glance down to find the orange tabby circling my feet, and I give a little squeal of fear as I do my best to shoo it.

"Oh no, you don't," I hiss. "Don't you go rubbing off that bad juju on me. I'm not interested in having a knife stab me in the back seven times." Even if that description isn't entirely accurate. I believe the coroner suggested there was at least one blow to the front, or was it two? Oh, I can't even think about it being out here alone in the dark with a ghost cat and—

It jerks a moment, tipping his head up to look at me with those large, watery, lantern green eyes.

"Oh my heaven." I melt as I bend over and give it a scratch behind its supernatural ears. "Yes, you sure are precious."

A thought strikes me. What if that's Mora in there that Travis just had that explosive argument with? What in the world would Mora Anne have to argue with him about so passionately?

Those cryptic words she spoke about her family stealing what's hers comes crashing back to me.

Was Mora seeing Travis first? Can't be. Merilee would never do that to her sister, would she? I mean, sure, they were sour apples to the rest of society, but alone they had a wonderful relationship, didn't they? I freeze solid as it all comes together. Could Merilee have stabbed Mora Anne in the back like that? And could Mora Anne have quite literally returned the favor?

Footsteps rustle in this direction coming from the orchard.

Holy heck, I need to get out of here. But she's close and my own feet don't seem willing to lead me to safety at the moment, so I do the only thing I can. I pull out my phone and text Noah.

Orchard. And hit send.

It's all I have time to say before Mora Anne is staring me in the face with that long, dark, stringy hair of hers, that pale skin that practically glows in the dark, that slit of a mouth that looks like a bloodstain.

"It was you," I say breathless. "You did it, didn't you?" The words come from me stunned as she backs me into the trees. "Why, Mora? Was Travis Darren really worth it?"

She shakes her head in disbelief. "You couldn't leave well enough alone, could you?" Her eyes widen, hot with rage. "You had to keep pushing and pushing. It wasn't good enough that you would never have been prosecuted for killing my sister. You simply found her. You had nothing to fear. But you're a ninny and you couldn't even figure that out."

Something next to her thigh catches a glimmer of moonlight, and as soon as I spot it, I can't seem to take my next breath. A long, slender knife, big enough to butcher a deer with gleams by her side, and she raises it as if to allow me a further inspection.

"I had to bring it with me tonight just in case I saw her."

"Merilee?" My goodness, Mora Anne's sanity really has flown the coop.

"No, not Merilee, you idiot. My cousin."

"*Cascade*? Why would you want to hurt her?"

"Why would I want to hurt her?" she shouts so loud her voice echoes throughout the orchard. "Why would she want to hurt *me*?" she riots, and I can feel the blowback on my face.

I bump into the branches of an apple tree from behind and come to a full stop. A thicket of trees surrounds me in every direction. There's nowhere for me to go except past Mora.

"Nobody wants to hurt you." I slip my phone into my pocket, and I can feel it vibrating with a message as soon as I tuck it into my jeans.

"You want to hurt me. Admit it." Her voice shakes as she dances the knife between us. "Cascade wants her money. And as long as I'm alive, she can't have it. Because it's mine. My uncle left everything to me. That will she has is a fake. He would never intentionally give that brat a dime."

"But she's blood, right? Maybe he changed his mind?"

A crazed cackle bounces from her. "I'm so darn tired of my relatives changing their minds." She shifts from foot to foot as if acting it out.

"Is that what happened? With Merilee? She changed her mind and didn't want Coach Hagan anymore?"

She chokes on another laugh. "She never wanted him until I pointed out how attractive and astute he was.

Merilee could never see the good in anyone for herself. She was too consumed trying to keep me boxed in by that shut-in lifestyle she demanded we have. And once she started to date, I thought I could too, so I found a gentleman of my own. But no"—silver tracks stream down her face as tears make their way to the ground—"she decided she liked Travis better and set out to seduce him herself. She convinced me to *wait* until my wedding day, but all the while she was using everything she had in her arsenal to secure Travis for herself. They spent afternoons sleeping together at the Evergreen while I worked to the bone at The Busy Bee." She lifts the knife and wipes the tears from her face with the back of her hand. "Sleeping together! She just put herself out there like some common street whore just to keep me from being happy." Her voice ticks up in a violent manner, her words garbled with agony. And as much as my heart breaks for her, I can't seem to take my eyes off the shiny blade of that knife she's wielding.

"Why would you kill her, though? And here at the orchard on one of their busiest days instead of somewhere secluded?"

She scoffs at the accusation. "You think I set out to kill my own sister? I was raging for months. And, believe me, I've thought about how much easier this life would be without her. I wanted her gone for a very long time, but not even I thought I could do it. And in a way, I didn't. All I remember is that Coach Hagan's wife came by and had it out with her. Told both my sister and me to stay out of her family right in front of Eve, that ridiculous book lady, and the mayor's wife. It was ugly and humiliating. Once they left, I had no choice but to confront my sister. I told her she needed to leave the coach once and for all. And that's when she informed me she had already left him. She was committing to Travis. *My* Travis. I told her she needed to leave him alone, that he was mine. But she just laughed and said she would get a proposal out of him by midnight. I just saw red. And the next thing I knew, I had a knife just like this one in my hand, and I was standing over my sister's dead body. I dropped the knife and ran into the restroom. I was hysterical after that."

I look to her hand and note the fact she's wearing her signature long black gloves. "That's why forensics couldn't place you as the killer. No prints. You wore gloves." A dull laugh pumps from me because I'm guessing she didn't plan that brilliant move. "You killed your sister, yes, but it was a crime of passion. You were in a rage. I'm positive a judge and jury will take that into account. You can tell them all about how abusive Merilee was to you."

"No!" she shouts so loud my entire body flinches.

Mora Anne raises the knife above her head. "It's over for you, Lottie. I'm the one who's sorry now. If you weren't so darn nosy, none of this would have happened. You could have lived for years cuddled up to that stupid furball of yours."

My adrenaline hits its zenith. "Nobody calls Pancake stupid." My foot sweeps the leaves she's standing on, sending both her and the knife sailing to the ground. I seize the moment and try to make a run for it, but Mora snatches me by the ankle and reels me back in.

"Let go." I buck and kick wildly as she snatches the knife back up and wields it with aggression.

This is the moment where I should probably scream my head off, but in reality it's taking way too much energy to even think about. Besides, I need every last bit of it so I can do this—

I reach forward and clasp my hand over her wrist as the knife dangles precariously over my head.

"Stop this right now, Mora!" I howl into her. "I'll tell the sheriff to go easy on you. It doesn't have to end this way."

"*You* end this way!" Her voice rises into the night sky as she breaks free from my grasp, and the knife drops to the ground with an unceremonious thump.

With all of my might I flip her onto her back and kick my knee into her gut as hard as I can.

Mora attempts to groan, but the wind seems to be knocked out of her and the only sound emitting from her throat is a dull croak.

I hop to my feet and step away from her, snatching the knife from a pile of leaves and breathing a sigh of relief. It's over. I have the knife, and I'm safe. I turn to look at her one last time, and my own feet are knocked out from underneath me and the knife violently snatched from my hand.

"Two can play at that game." She laughs. "You don't get to walk out of here tonight, Lottie." The knife comes down fast just above my chest, and I roll to my right as it plunges into the ground.

"Crap!" I try to roll away from her, but she's on me and we're wrestling once again, that knife diving around my head and chest as if it were alive.

"Lottie!" Noah's deep voice resonates from behind and Mora looks over. I push my elbow up and hit her square in the face, shutting her mouth by way of her chin with a loud, satisfying pop.

"*Lottie*!" Noah roars as he pulls Mora Anne off me. "She's over here!" he shouts behind him, and an entire fleet of deputies stream in to subdue her.

Noah helps me to my feet, and I stumble backwards until we're embedded between a pair of trees laden with fruit. The moon shines down over the orchard like a spotlight, and Noah glows with a silent rage that's quickly diminishing to something just this side of relief.

"Why would you openly go against the captain's orders?" His voice is firm, yet layered with caring underneath.

"Why would you demand I listen to you like you're some authority figure in my life and I'm your subordinate?" I shout right back.

"I was trying to keep you alive!"

"Well, I wasn't trying to die on purpose!" I pause for a moment, still trying to catch my breath. "Okay, so as far as comebacks go, that was pretty lame. But you just sailed into my life, so obnoxious in everything you said and did. And don't you even get me started on that ego! You think every woman on the planet lives to—"

"Kiss me," he says as his cheeks twitch with the hint of a

smile. And just like that, he presses those lips of his to mine and doesn't break the seal for a solid ten seconds and neither do I. He pulls back, and I can still feel his chest pounding just as hard as mine. "You scared me." His voice wavers a moment. "Don't do that again. Please," he adds softly, and a tiny smile flickers on my face.

"Kiss me again and I'll consider it."

He sheds that signature cocky grin as he takes me in like this. From over his shoulder I spot a shimmering orange ball of light move deep into the orchard in the shape of a beautiful little tabby. Its tail waves in the air as it takes off, and its body becomes clear as night until its all but evaporated.

Noah lands his lips to mine one more time, and I grab him by the neck and press him in. I want to feel him, feel everything.

I survived. Merilee's killer was caught in the most unfortunate manner, after exposing the most unfortunate circumstances. And I'm alive, standing here with gorgeous Detective Noah Fox with his heart drumming up against mine.

Maybe, just maybe, there is someone out there who has the capability to want me in their life exclusively, perhaps even forever.

Maybe, just maybe, that person is right here in front of me.

I think he is.

CHAPTER 17

Fall in Honey Hollow comes in phases. First, there is the inkling of a cool breeze alerting summer that her seasonal duties are coming to an end. Next, comes the crisp, autumn wind that blows the dying leaves in all of their colorful splendor around town like confetti as the town itself becomes a parade of beauty on display for the world to admire. Finally, the frost becomes a permanent fixture as the season itself dies just like those leaves it so celebrated. The baton is passed to winter, and all things are once again discovered anew.

And just like fall, one of my favorite seasons of the year, I too feel as if I came into my own right along with it. I had never realized how much I held onto the failures of the past, the rejection, the abandonment that plagues me had all become etched over my soul like a badge of dishonor, and unbeknownst to me I had worn it with pleasure. I think it's time to remove the badge, remove the shame and the disgrace that others have inflicted, that I may have inflicted on myself. It's time to discover a new version of who I am and all that I can be. Time, in fact, has been my greatest teacher, ushering me through each new phase of my being. The metamorphosis continues as I stretch my wings and fly, as I fly so high I touch the stratosphere with the new opportunities presented to me. And I look forward to each new discovery as I lift the boulders of the past off my spirit, brush the dust off myself, and enter into the light of this new life. It is a beautiful, beautiful thing to realize that you are not defined by who you once were, that life is ever-evolving around you, and that you, in fact, are along for the magical ride.

A lot has happened in Honey Hollow this past month, and in order to move on from what was, Nell has decided to host an open house at the Honey Pot. All day and well into the evening, residents have been streaming as a show of community, to show the world that we are indeed family, that we are strong and celebrate one another's victories, and just as easily mourn one another's defeats. No one is pleased that Mora Anne had a terrible life with her sister. Certainly an emotional imprisonment like the one Merilee imposed on her was painful to hear about and process. But we are all relieved that Mora Anne will get the help she needs. The psychological examination proved that the assistance she requires will be extensive although not impossible to achieve. Everett says she will most likely be sent to a place where there is a hospital-like environment, and each day she will work to restore herself, the true self she lost way back when all of that emotional abuse began. I've already resolved to visit her whenever possible. Yes, she tried very hard to kill me, but I believe in second chances and during her arrest Mora Anne has already quite sincerely apologized profusely.

And per the rumor mill, as led by its most active member, my mother, Coach Hagan and his wife are officially in counseling. There's no telling if they will ever truly restore what was lost, but at least they will be civil to one another for the sake of their children.

Travis Darren, as rumor and confirmation of said rumor would have it, is now dating Naomi Turner's best friend, Lily Swanson. Once word spread on the street that Travis was a well sought-after man, a fair amount of ladies turned up the volume and strutted their stuff in front of the leaf peeping guide. He had a bevy of beauties to choose from, and he happily chose the shallowest of them all. I suppose, in the end, he too received his just desserts.

My mother has confided in me that both Eve Hollister and Chrissy Nash have taken a personal vow to never withhold anything juicy from her again. She really leveraged that whole my-daughter's-life-was-in-the-balance thing, and, suffice it to say, she will never be in the proverbial dark again.

Keelie wraps an arm around me as we stare out at all the bodies circulating through the Honey Pot. There's a buffet set up on the wall adjacent to what will be the official new bakery, and appropriately enough there are desserts for every and anyone who would like to partake. I gladly lost myself in the kitchen after that entire horror at the orchard. I still have nightmares about that steely blade slashing around my head and wake up gasping for air, so Pancake has taken up permanent residency on my pillow as opposed to near my feet where he usually slept. And those nightmares are becoming fewer and fewer. I couldn't have asked for a better furry guardian angel.

"So, what do you think?" Keelie asks as she looks to the crowd. "Did Honey Hollow survive its first great tragedy?"

"Are you kidding? We not only survived, we're thriving."

Mom comes up with a suppressed look of joy on her face as she lunges at me with a firm embrace. "I couldn't agree more." She pulls back, that bright red smile of hers expanding for more. "And you, my little girl"—she pinches my cheek with vigor—"are thriving, too." There's a sparkle in her eyes that's saying something more than just her words imply, and a part of me doesn't understand it just yet, but I know that in time I will. All will be known. And we will undoubtedly know so much more than we could ever carry or comprehend at the moment.

Lainey pops up behind her, the ever-dutiful Tanner Redwood ambling by her side. "Just stay out of trouble from now on, would you? And for the love of all things sane, do not stumble upon another dead body. It only leads to trouble."

"I agree on all points. And though it was unspoken, I just want you to know that I'm already looking for a new place to live. So you don't have to worry about me living in your guest room forever."

"*What?*" Her cheeks pique with color, a cute little attribute my sister has had for as long as I can remember once she gets flustered. "You do not have to do that. You know I love having you around. And who will I share goodnight kisses with if Pancake isn't there to tuck me in? I won't have it. But if you insist, at least take your time. My door will always be open to you."

"Thank you. I very much appreciate that."

The three of them proceed to the dessert table, and my mother is grabbing as many people as she can on the way over, forming a conga line while she's at it.

"Forever the life of the party," I point out to Keelie.

"I am, aren't I?" a deep voice rumbles from our left, and we turn to find the delectable, delicious, and, might I add, dapper Detective Noah Fox.

"*Noah*!" I wrap my arms around him and indulge in a relatively tame kiss. We'll get to the untamed kisses as soon as we're alone. Noah has been a rock of support over the last few dizzying days, and we've come to terms with who we are as people. He's accepted me for the strong-willed, strong-minded, and very much competent to keep myself safe woman I am. And I've accepted his unrelenting praise and affection. It is very hard for someone like me, who has received her fair share of rejection over the course of my twenty-six years, to come to terms with the fact there are some people who simply will not reject you, and if they do, that's on them. I will be just fine, regardless. I don't need everyone to love and accept me. I need the love and acceptance of those who are willing to give it. It's a game of give and take. And I choose to give as much love and acceptance to those around me to make up for lost time as well.

"Enough already with the PDA," another male voice grumbles, and we cease and desist our love-fest only to find Everett standing there with a genuine grin blooming on his face. A cup of cider rests in his hand, and he looks relaxed, happy even. "You two look good together." That smile of his does a quick exit. "And I'm happy that I've gotten to know you, Lemon." He nods my way before looking to his once upon a time stepbrother. "And I'm"—he looks to Noah a good long while—"I'm glad we didn't throw punches." He lifts his mug, and I can tell there is still work to do as far as restoration goes between these two.

Keelie points toward the tree in the center of the establishment, and we find Nell tapping the edge of a glass with a knife as she calls the room to attention. The twinkle lights that wrap around the trunk of the tree and spray out over the branches covering the ceiling give this place a magical glow that someplace as magical as the Honey Pot Diner deserves.

"Attention, please, attention," Nell shouts as she commands the room. "I just wanted to say that it is my great pleasure to host our fine community—a community of love and inclusion, a safe place for all. Where, there might be a few that are blood-related—we are all indeed family. Please enjoy the sweet treats baked by my granddaughter, Lottie Lemon." She gives a playful wink my way, and my heart sings when she calls me that. It always does. "In fact, it is also my great pleasure to announce that through the careful greasing of the right hands, my new venture that I have embarked upon with my granddaughter, Lottie, is about to come to fruition. The Cutie Pie Bakery and Cakery, which will include fine confections, gourmet coffee, and more, will be conveniently located right next door in just a few weeks."

Keelie nudges me with her elbow. "She said *cakery*. I think she added that part."

"I know," I whisper back, amused. "But you know what? It works, and I think I really like it. I know I do. And this way, it's both Nell and me who got to name it." I melt at the thought of something so sweet transpiring so organically.

"So, everyone"—Nell cries out—"enjoy the food, enjoy all the season has to bring, and most of all, enjoy each other. As we have tragically seen, this life and all it has to offer can be all too short." Nell wraps up her speech by way of lifting her cider, and the room does the same before breaking out into applause.

Keelie tugs at my arm. "Come on. Let's go next door and see this wonder that *our* grandmother has bestowed upon you." She gives a cheeky wink of her own because she would love nothing more than to have me as a genuine part of the family and, in a way that supersedes blood, we already are.

Noah, Everett, and I stroll next door with her and look into the oversized windows as Bear and Hunter put the finishing touches on what will soon be my second home. Who am I kidding? It will be my true home. The place my heart will be happiest and at true rest, baking. The autumn chill arrests us with its icy fingers as the maple leaves race over to our feet in colors of ruby and carrot, the colors of bittersweet wine.

Hunter gives a quick wave and slaps Bear over the shoulder as he points our way before both men come out to join us.

Hunter grins, looking every bit like his cousin in the process. "You ready to throw a party once this place opens up for business?"

"A party?" I startle at the thought.

"Yup," Bear agrees with his cousin with a nod. "You need to christen this place with friends and family. I accept a full brownie bar in my honor." That ear-to-ear grin of his blooms once again, and something in me finds Bear a little more tolerable than I ever have before. I suppose since today is a day of forgiveness, and moving on from the past—well, I choose to do just that between Bear and me and let go of all of my emotional grievances against him.

I look to Everett and Noah, and they both give a thumbs-up at the idea of a party.

"I guess I'll be having a grand opening!" I look to Bear. "And I will most certainly have *Bear's Brownie Bar* open for one and all. I can't thank you enough for making this project a priority."

Keelie grasps my hand a moment. "And Nell for greasing his Bear claw."

"Nell for sure," I say as Noah wraps his arms around me from behind, and I lean against him, the two of us looking into the bakery as if we could see the future and all of the delicious things it holds for us.

Keelie presses a hand against the glass. "We're going to kill it."

A small laugh breaks out as Bear and Hunter head back in and get to work once again.

Keelie sighs. "Okay, so in light of everything that's transpired, I will definitely rethink my language." She looks to me and winks. "But you are going to slay this town with this bakery and don't you for a minute doubt yourself. Best of all, I get to see you do it. Front row seats right here at the Honey Pot." She gives a wave of the fingertips before skipping off next door once again.

Everett gives a slight bow my way. "Lemon, I can't wait for the invite. I know you'll do this town proud." He takes in an enormous breath as he looks to Noah. "Thank you for sharing with me what you've done. I won't spoil the surprise. It looks as if Noah Fox is one of the good guys after all." Everett pins his gaze to mine once again and holds it there. His blue eyes exude an unspoken sadness, a touch of grief that transports from him to me. "You're a pretty great person yourself, Lemon." He takes off for the Honey Pot, and we watch until the door closes behind him.

I spin around in Noah's arms and look up at this handsome man who crashed through the ceiling of my life and somehow became an important fixture in it.

"What's the surprise? Am I getting a surprise?" My mouth opens with a smile. Noah has been one surprise after the next ever since I became aware of his existence.

"In a strange way, I've already given it to you." His shoulders bounce, making him look both vexingly sexy and humble all at the same time. "Turn around."

I spin in his arms once again, and he tightens his hold over me, his chin resting on my shoulder. "Remember that day you blew into my office like a hurricane and kindly asked for a loan for kitchen equipment?"

"How can I forget? My ego is still bruised from the effort," I tease. "I'd like to think it were fate or kismet that the loan department needed an overhaul. Because if it didn't, I probably wouldn't have you in my life."

"Well, that might be true. And you might have had to find another way to get your kitchen appliances."

I turn back around, completely baffled. "Meaning?"

He winces as if what came next was almost painful to admit. "Meaning I gave you the loan. But it's not a loan. It's a gift from me to you."

"*What?*" I try to take a step back, but he's still holding

me tight. "Did you give Nell the money to buy the appliances? I'm sorry. I'm so confused. You lost me."

"The truth is, I asked Nell to keep it a secret. You see, I had come into some money not long after my father had died. It was a sizeable sum, but I didn't want any of it. It was mostly money that he pilfered and conned other people out of, even though my father was a shrewd businessman in his own right. Nevertheless, I tried my hardest to give back what he took from my stepmother, but she wouldn't have it. That's when I had an idea. I gave you the money, Lottie. I didn't see a reason your dream should be delayed, and this way you don't have the burden of a loan. And it's not a loan. It's a gift, Lottie. I wanted you to have it. I hope it brings you many years of happiness."

"*Noah,*" I whisper, unable to catch my breath. "I don't know what to say." I shake my head, my gaze unable to break from his. "This is unbelievable. Are you sure you want me to have that much of your father's estate? Maybe we can set up a payment schedule, and as soon as possible I can start paying you back."

"No." He laughs at the thought. "That, I will not allow. It's simply yours. Enjoy it. I spoke to Everett about it afterwards, and he agreed it was best."

Tears come to my eyes as I take him in. "Well then. Thank you from the bottom of my heart. You are just as gorgeous of a man on the inside as you are on the outside, and I feel privileged and humbled by your decision." I bite down on my lower lip. "I think this qualifies you for free sweets for life." I hike my shoulder up at him. "And I won't take no for an answer."

"In that case, I guess my answer is yes."

"Good." I wrap my arms around his neck. "And I hope the answer to the next question is yes as well. Kiss me?"

His whole face erupts into a greedy grin. "Always a yes to that, Lottie Lemon."

Noah's lips fall to mine, and we indulge in another act of sinfully delicious affection, this time with far more attention to the tasks at hand. Noah Fox and his superhuman lips melt me in the most spectacular way. My head spins from the dizzying effect, and it feels as if he's holding me up to keep me from slipping away from existence entirely. Noah and I are just at the beginning of what could be something special, and it will be no matter what happens next.

There is so much hope, so much more to do and see in Honey Hollow. A grand opening for the bakery and all of the Halloween and fall festivities that October brings are almost upon us.

For once everything in my life seems to be headed in the right direction, moving at a perfectly arced trajectory toward the mark of a beautiful, beautiful future.

For the life of me, I can't imagine what could possibly go wrong.

. . .

*****NEED more Honey Hollow? Read the next book today! Click here—> Bobbing for Bodies (Murder in the Mix 2) and read NOW!**

*Be sure to **subscribe to Addison's mailing list** for sneak peeks and updates on all upcoming releases!

My name is Lottie Lemon, and I see dead people. Okay, so rarely do I see dead people. Mostly I see furry creatures of the dearly departed variety, who have come

back from the other side to warn me of their previous owner's impending doom.

Trust me when I say this is not a good sign. So, when I spot an adorable, fuzzy, little squirrel skipping around at the grand opening for my new bakery, I about lose it, until I realize it's a perky little poltergeist only visible to yours truly. But there are so many people at the grand opening it's hard to discern who exactly might be in danger—that is, until I follow the little creature right out the back and straight into another homicide. It's horrible to see your friend lying there vacant of life. Honey Hollow will never be the same.

LOTTIE LEMON HAS a brand new bakery to tend to, a budding romance with perhaps one too many suitors, and she has the supernatural ability to see dead pets—which are always harbingers for ominous things to come. Throw in the occasional ghost of the human variety, a string of murders, and her insatiable thirst for justice, and you'll have more chaos than you know what to do with.

Living in the small town of Honey Hollow can be murder.

Pick up Bobbing for Bodies (Murder in the Mix 2) available NOW!

PREVIEW: Bobbing for Bodies (Murder in the Mix 2)

I see dead people.

It's true. I do see dead people on occasion, but it's mostly cute, fuzzy, creatures that hop over from the other side to say hello—and, believe me, it's never a good sign for whoever they've come to greet. But, at the moment, I'm not looking at a ghastly phantasm. No, this is no ghost, and as much as I hate to admit it, she very much feels like a harbinger of ominous things to come.

The tiny metal newsstand that sits in front of the Honey Pot Diner has Merilee Simonson's face staring back at me from behind the glass. It was just last month that Honey Hollow had its very first homicide, and I was unlucky enough to discover the body. Merilee, my old landlord, was even unluckier to *be* the body.

I shake all thoughts of that hairy scary day out of my mind as I step out into the street to admire the newly minted bakery which Nell, my best friend's grandmother and my boss by proxy, has put me in charge of.

"The Cutie Pie Bakery and Cakery," I whisper as I take in the beauty of the divine little shop that I've gleefully been holing up in the last week solid while baking up a storm for today's grand opening. It's the beginning of October, and autumn is showing off all of its glory in our little corner of Vermont. Honey Hollow is famous for its majestic thickets of ruby maples, liquidambars, and bright yellow birch trees—all of the above with leaves in every color of the citrine rainbow. The sweet scent of cinnamon rolls baking, heady vanilla, and the thick scent of robust coffee permeate all of Main Street, incapacitating residents and tourists alike, forcing them to stagger down toward the bakery in a hypnotic state. I'm pretty sure I won't need business cards to pull in the masses. I'll opt for the olfactory takedown every single time. Not even the heavy fog that is rolling down the street this morning has the power to subdue those heavenly scents.

Hunter, my notorious ex-boyfriend's cousin, stretches to life as he stands from where he was crouching by the entry. Bear and Hunter have been working out in front for the last three days trying to repair cracks in the wall that divides this place from Nell's original restaurant, the Honey Pot Diner. Inside, a nice opening has been made in the south-facing wall so that patrons of both establishments can meander from place to place. And I'm glad about it, too. I've been a baker at the Honey Pot for so long I would have missed seeing the inner workings of it daily even though it is right next door. Not to mention the fact my best friend, Keelie, is the manager at the Honey Pot, so this guarantees I'll still see her smiling face each and every morning.

Hunter strides over and rests his elbow over my shoulder as we take in the sight together.

"Don't forget that part," he says, pointing to the smaller sign below the words I just read. "Fine confections, gourmet coffee, and more!" he reads it just as enthusiastically as the exclamation point suggests.

We share a little laugh, never taking our eyes off the place. Otis *Bear* Fisher—the aforementioned and somewhat infamous ex—and Hunter spent all last week getting the furniture for the bakery painted in every shade of pastel. Bear bought out all of the chairs and café tables he could find at his friend's chain of secondhand stores, and the end result is so sweet and cozy it's hard for me to leave this place at night.

"Thank you for all your hard work," I say, looking up at Bear's lookalike cousin. After Bear shattered my heart into shards as if it were a haunted mirror, it was Hunter who offered up his support and suggested I leave town for a bit to clear my head. I took his advice and hightailed it to New York—Columbia University to be exact—and, well, let's just say my heart was shattered ten times harder in the big city than it ever was in Honey Hollow. "You know, I've probably never said this before, but thank you for your friendship, too." I can't help but sniff back tears. "You really have been a rock in my life. I'm sorry I didn't get a chance to tell you sooner." I offer a quick embrace to the surly blond with the body of a brick building. Both Bear and Hunter look as if they're primed to be lumberjacks with their tree-like muscles, but lucky for me their chosen profession just so happens to be construction.

"Whoa, easy, Lottie. Don't shed a single tear for me." He laughs at the thought. "I know this day is an emotional one for you. This bakery has been your destiny for as long as I can remember." He nods back to the place where his tools are strewn all over the sidewalk just under the scaffolding he's had set up for days to assist him in the exhausting effort. "Let me clean this mess up so you can get your party started." He jogs back to the sprawl of tools, and I quickly follow him under the canopy of this skeletal structure.

"It's not bad luck to stand under a scaffolding, is it?" I

tease. I'll admit, my nerves are slightly jangled just thinking about the festivities about to ensue.

He barks out a short-lived laugh. "Nope, that would be a ladder. But you're not allowed to have any bad luck, period. This is your big day, Lottie Lemon, and I promise you not one thing will go wrong." He gives a playful wink, and something about that facial disclaimer sends me in a jittery panic ten times more than before. He winces. "I think I left something out back."

Hunter takes off, and no sooner does he leave than I press my hand to the window of the bakery, a no-no as far as Keelie is concerned. She's been helping me scrub and scour every inch of this place to get it ready for its big debut, but I'll gladly wipe away my own fingerprints in a moment just to garner one more look inside before we open. It's all there—the café tables and chairs look as sweet as confections themselves, the refrigerated shelves that line the front are fully stocked and loaded with every cookie, brownie, and delicious dessert you can think of, and the walls are painted a decadent shade of butter yellow. My sister, Lainey, came by yesterday to help me decorate the place for Halloween with ghosts, witches, and scarecrows set in every free space. Autumn leaves carefully line the counters, and tiny orange pumpkins dot each table with gold and red maple leaves blooming out from underneath them. To think that in just a few short hours this place will be filled with family and friends—with Everett and Noah. Noah who—

A horrible creaking sound comes from the scaffolding

above me, and I look up in time to see the gargantuan structure rocking back and forth. My entire body freezes solid as it careens toward me, and before I know it, I'm hit from behind by a warm body, pushed to safety as the entire scaffolding crashes into a pile of dust. That metal newspaper stand is lying on its side, and Merilee's grinning face is staring back up at me in replicate.

"Oh my word," I pant as I struggle to catch my breath.

"Geez, lady." A man with dark curly hair, a lantern jaw, and eyes the color of espresso pats me down by the shoulders. "You okay? You almost got crushed to death." His eyes widen a notch at the thought as do mine.

"Yeah"—I glance down at my body, thankfully still intact—"I'm fine. You saved my life!" My hand clutches at the thought of me dying, right here in front of my own bakery on opening day of all occasions. How horrible that would have been for me and perhaps for all of Honey Hollow, considering there is a stockpile of sweet treats in there to feed the entire community for a month if need be. I'd hate to think that anyone would let all of my hard work go to waste just because I met an untimely demise, but I suppose seeing my body splattered like a dead fly might kill an appetite or two. "You have to come inside." I grip him by the sleeve, and he quickly frees himself with a shake of the head. "Please, let me give you a cake or something. You're a *hero*!"

"I'm no hero." He glances past my shoulder just as Hunter and Bear shout their way over. "I gotta run. I got a kid waiting for me at home." He jogs across the street and is swallowed up by the fog within two seconds.

"*Wait*," I call after him. "Please bring your family by later! We're having a party!"

"Lottie!" Bear pulls me in tight, and I struggle to breathe for a moment before inching away. "You could have been killed!" He turns his attention back to the carnage. "*Hunter*" —he barks—"how many times have I told you not to put heavy crap on top of the scaffolding?" he riots over at his cousin, and poor Hunter looks just as shaken as I do.

"I didn't. I swear." He kicks one of the hefty looking bags that almost crushed me right along with the planks on that scaffolding. "I'd never put bags of quick-set on there. I'm not that *insane*," he riots right back.

Keelie appears from nowhere and pulls me into the safety of the Cutie Pie Bakery.

"Don't you worry about a thing, girl." She slings her svelte arm around my shoulder as we take in this magical place, and somehow the trauma of what I've just been through begins to subside. "It's a good thing to get all of the bad luck out of the way up front." She bites down on a ruby red lip as if it isn't. Keelie and I bonded at an early age, and she's felt every bit like one of my sisters. Her blonde curls are pulled back into a ponytail, and her bright blue eyes glow as if someone lit a match behind them. Keelie is as peppy as she is sincere, and I love every attribute about her. "This is one of the best days of your life, and I never want you to forget a single moment of it. It's nothing but good luck from here on out."

"Right," I say, looking past my bubbly bestie, and with everything in me I want to believe her. "Nothing but good luck."

I glance back outside as Hunter and Bear work to clean up the debris. It's so windy those newspapers have come apart and are floating through the air like ghosts.

Then with a slap, the front page of one of those papers seals itself against the glass, and there she is, Merilee Simonson and her unnatural grimace looking right at me like a dark omen as if to say *there will be nothing good about this day.*

There is not one part of me that believes Keelie's kind words. There will be no good luck today.

Something tells me it will be bad, bad, bad.

*****Need more Honey Hollow? Click here—> Bobbing for Bodies (Murder in the Mix 2) and read NOW!**

NEW YORK TIMES BESTSELLER
ADDISON MOORE
MURDER
IN THE MIX
Bobbing For
Bodies

RECIPE

From the kitchen of the Cutie Pie Bakery and Cakery

Lottie's Cutie Pies

Hello friend, Lottie Lemon here! I hope you enjoyed your visit to Honey Hollow. Fall is not only the best time to stop by our quirky little town but it just so happens to be my favorite season. Here's the recipe to my bakery's namesake cutie pies. It does have a number of steps but I promise it's well worth the effort. I really hope you enjoy these pies.

Hope to see you back in Honey Hollow real soon! Happy baking!

***Note: This pie crust requires an overnight chill time**

in the fridge or, in a pinch, 4 hours of chilling in the freezer will do.

***Note #2** Instead of using a standard 9" pie pan this recipe calls for two 5" pans. You can pick up disposable pie tins in this size, by the dozen, online or in the baking section of your local grocery store. If you'd rather use one 9" pan you can do that as well.

You can also use store-bought dough to make the pies. I promise they will be just as delicious!

Pie Crust

Ingredients

2 ½ cups all-purpose flour
½ teaspoon salt
1 cup chilled butter (cubed)
½ cup ice water

Directions

Just prior to using the dough, preheat oven to 375°

In a large mixing bowl combine flour and salt, then cut in butter until mixture is crumbly. Add ice water a bit at a time until dough forms a firm ball. Wrap in plastic or place in covered bowl and refrigerate overnight (or 4 hours in the freezer if you're in a pinch).

Divide dough into 4 equal pieces.

Roll out all 4 pieces into circles to about 1/8 of an inch to fit two 5 inch pie pans.

At this point you're going to want to blind bake 2 of your pie crusts so that the bottom of your pie isn't soggy or undercooked when your pie is ready to eat. This process is super simple. (Keep two of the circles refrigerated during this process. You can keep them from drying out by covering them with parchment paper, top and bottom.)

Place your dough into the pie pans and press your edges in a decorative manner. I like to crimp the dough around the periphery so that it has a nice scalloped edge.

Take a fork and poke holes into the bottom and sides of the dough to prevent bubbling.

Place the pie pans into the freezer for 10-15 minutes to get the butter to firm up once again and keep the dough from losing shape in the oven.

Place a layer of parchment paper over the bottom of your pie and extending up over the sides. Fill the center of the pie with dry beans or rice.

Bake shell for 10 minutes. Carefully remove the parchment and the beans or rice. Place back in the oven for 10 minutes.

Caramel Sauce

Ingredients

1 cup of sugar

6 tablespoons unsalted butter (salted if you'd like your caramel to have a savory tang)

½ cup heavy cream

Directions

Pour sugar into a medium-size saucepan over a medium to low heat. Stir constantly until sugar melts, brown and bubbling. Quickly add butter and stir until butter is completely melted. *Use caution when adding the butter! The melted sugar will bubble extra once the butter is added. I like to wear long sleeves or gloves when doing this step. Keep stirring constantly and slowly add heavy cream. Once cream is added let sit for about 1 minute while boiling once again. Bubbling mixture will rise in the pan.

Turn off stove and place saucepan onto a cooling rack until close to room temperature.

*Note: Keelie likes to cheat in this area and use store-bought caramel sauce, and there's no shame in her cheating game. Feel free to follow suit if you like! You can easily find caramel sauce around the ice cream section of the grocery store.

Apple Filling

Ingredients

8 medium or 7 large apples, (any kind you prefer) peeled, cored, and sliced thin. ½ cup of sugar

2 tablespoons lemon juice

½ cup flour

1 teaspoon vanilla

¼ teaspoon ground cloves

¼ teaspoon ground nutmeg

2 teaspoons ground cinnamon

1 egg (for use in washing the crust to give it that shiny glow)

2 tablespoons milk (for egg wash)

*handful of chopped walnuts optional. About ¼ cup.

Directions for Apple Filling and putting together our *Cutie Pies*!

Preheat oven to 400°

In a large bowl add apple slices, lemon, sugar, flour, cloves, nutmeg, cinnamon, and vanilla. If you've decided to use the chopped walnuts, add them during this step.

Fold together all ingredients with a spatula until well combined. Fill the two pie pans with the apple mixture (inside of the crust that has been blind baked).

*Drizzle ¼ cup of caramel into each pie (You'll want to

save the rest of the caramel to drizzle over individual slices. Trust me, this will be amazing.)

Carefully place the uncooked circles of dough over the top of the pie and crimp the top crust along the rim of the pie pan. With a sharp knife cut four slices (1 inch each) into the center of the pie crust, an equal distance from one another.

Note: You can also get fancy and weave a lattice with the top pie crust if you wish. With a sharp knife, slice the uncooked crust into ½ inch strips. Alternate laying strips horizontally and vertically weaving horizontal strips over and under the vertical.

Now is the perfect time to make the egg wash! See below.

Egg wash
Directions
Whisk together egg and 2 tablespoons milk.

With a baker's pastry brush (my preference is the silicone variety) or with a napkin rolled tight, dip into egg mixture and gently wash the top of the crust on both cutie pies.

Place pies onto a baking sheet and then into the oven.

Bake 40-45 minutes until apple mixture is bubbling.

Set pies out to cool for an hour or two.
Be sure to use your caramel reserves for extra drizzles.

Enjoy!

BOOKS BY ADDISON MOORE

Paranormal Women's Fiction

Hot Flash Homicides

Midlife in Glimmerspell

Wicked in Glimmerspell

Mistletoe in Glimmerspell

Cozy Mysteries

Cruising Through Midlife

Cruising Through Midlife

Mai Tai Murder Cruise

Hibiscus Homicide Cruise

Brambleberry bay Murder Club

Brambleberry Bay Murder Club

Cozy Mysteries

Meow for Murder

Murder at Mortimer Manor

Murder Old School

Socialite's Guide to Murder

Haunted Halloween Murder

Murder for Christmas

Murder Made Delicious

Marriage can be Murder

Country Cottage Mysteries

Kittyzen's Arrest

Dog Days of Murder

Santa Claws Calamity

Bow Wow Big House

Murder Bites

Felines and Fatalities

A Killer Tail

Cat Scratch Cleaver

Just Buried

Butchered After Bark

A Frightening Fangs-giving

A Christmas to Dismember

Sealed with a Hiss

A Winter Tail of Woe

Lock, Stock, and Feral

Itching for Justice

Raining Cats and Killers

Death Takes a Holiday

Copycat Killer Thriller

Happy Howl-o-ween Horror

Twas the Night Before Murder

Smitten Kitten Corruption

Cruising for Trouble

Beach Body

A Ruthless Ruff Patch

Murder in the Mix Mysteries

Cutie Pies and Deadly Lies

Bobbing for Bodies

Pumpkin Spice Sacrifice

Gingerbread & Deadly Dread

Seven-Layer Slayer

Red Velvet Vengeance

Bloodbaths and Banana Cake

New York Cheesecake Chaos

Lethal Lemon Bars

Macaron Massacre

Wedding Cake Carnage

Donut Disaster

Toxic Apple Turnovers

Killer Cupcakes

Pumpkin Pie Parting

Yule Log Eulogy

Pancake Panic

Sugar Cookie Slaughter

Devil's Food Cake Doom

Snickerdoodle Secrets

Strawberry Shortcake Sins

Cake Pop Casualties

Flag Cake Felonies

Peach Cobbler Confessions

Poison Apple Crisp

Spooky Spice Cake Curse

Pecan Pie Predicament

Eggnog Trifle Trouble

Waffles at the Wake

Raspberry Tart Terror

Baby Bundt Cake Confusion

Chocolate Chip Cookie Conundrum

Wicked Whoopie Pies

Key Lime Pie Perjury

Red, White, and Blueberry Muffin Murder

Honey Buns Homicide

Apple Fritter Fright

Vampire Brownie Bite Bereavement

Pumpkin Roll Reckoning

Cookie Exchange Execution

Heart-Shaped Confection Deception

Birthday Cake Bloodshed

Cream Puff Punishment

Last Rites Beignet Bites

Christmas Fudge Fatality

Mystery

Little Girl Lost

Never Say Sorry

The First Wife's Secret

For a full list please visit Addisonmoore.com

ACKNOWLEDGMENTS

A HUGE and hearty thank you to YOU, the reader, for diving into this new adventure with me. I hope you loved and adored Lottie and all of the Honey Hollow peeps as much as I did! This series has a very special place in my dark and twisted heart. I hope you'll join me on the next leg of the MURDER IN THE MIX adventure for more mayhem and mischief!

A spectacular thank you to Jodie Tarleton for blessing this book with your extraterrestrial vision. You really have an extraordinary knack, and without you this book would not be the same. You are my angel!

Thank you to the fabulous Kaila Eileen Turingan-Ramos, who brings it each and every time! You are a true ninja warrior with whom no missing word can contend. Love you!

A big, beautiful thank you to the sweetest of the sweet, Shay Rivera, for beta reading and pointing things out that I would never have seen without you. I know you will do amazing things in this wonderful life. You are a brilliant soul, and I am honored to know you!

Gushing running hugs to Lisa Markson. You're my safe place, and you know it.

To the real Keelie, thank you for sharing your beautiful presence with me and your beautiful name. I look forward to sharing real adventures with you.

A special thank you to Lou Harper at Cover Affairs for making this cover unbelievably beautiful!

All of my love and thanks to my amazing sister, Paige Maroney Smith, who is fierce and lovely and wise. You are truly family to me. A simple thank you is not enough for what you do. I love you!

And last, but never least, thank you to Him who sits on the throne. Worthy is the Lamb! Glory and honor and power are yours. I owe you everything, Jesus.

ABOUT THE AUTHOR

Addison Moore is a ***New York Times, USA Today,*** and ***Wall Street Journal*** bestselling author who writes contemporary and paranormal romance. Her work has been featured in ***Cosmopolitan*** Magazine. Previously she worked as a therapist on a locked psychiatric unit for nearly a decade. She resides on the West Coast with her husband, four wonderful children, and two dogs where she eats too much chocolate and stays up way too late. When she's not writing, she's reading. Addison's Celestra Series has been optioned for film by **20th Century Fox.**

Made in the USA
Columbia, SC
24 June 2024